Hope

Mike Phelps

Storms At Kendiamong

Copyright © 2015 Michael L. Phegley

All rights reserved. No part of this book may be reproduced, stored, or transmitted by any means whether auditory, graphic, mechanical, or electronic without written permission of the author, except in the case of brief excerpts used in critical articles and reviews. Unauthorized reproduction of any part of this work is illegal and punishable by Law. ISBN 978-0-9969691-0-9.

As an author I am interested in the opinions of my readers. Why did you read the book? What parts did you like or dislike? Would you like to hear more of this story? The answers to these questions and any other criticism you choose to share will help me in preparation of the sequel now being written.

Contact the author at stormsatkendiamong@gmail.com.

Michael L. Phegley

STORMS AT KENDIAMONG

Joe-Pye Press
200 Hanover drive Evansville IN

Table of Contents

Introduction iii
Disclosure iv
Definitions v
Spelling vi
Distances and Maps vii
Acknowledgments viii
Special Thanks ix
Dedication x
Preface xi

Chapter 1: Morning in the Valley 2
Chapter 2: The War Cry 5
Chapter 3: The Strangers 9
Chapter 4: The News 12
Chapter 5: Supper 17
Chapter 6: The Farm 20
Chapter 7: The Mission 26
Chapter 8: The River 28
Chapter 9: To the Susquehanna 35
Chapter 10: Coshecton 39
Chapter 11: The Blacksmith 50
Chapter 12: The Run-away 55
Chapter 13: The Hatchet 58
Chapter 14: The Iroquois 65
Chapter 15: The Christenings 70
Chapter 16: The Dutch Church with a Roof 79
Chapter 17: Jaol 84
Chapter 18: Home at the Mill 91
Chapter 19: March 1750 95
Chapter 20: Night Ride 101
Chapter 21: The Shadow Of Death 104
Chapter 22: Solomon the Third 109
Chapter 23: Peters Point 114
Chapter 24: War 124
Chapter 25: Braddock's Defeat 128

Chapter 26: The Fort 132
Chapter 27: Gnadenhutten...139
Chapter 28: Brink's Fort 142
Chapter 29: Headquarters New Jersey Frontier 1755 145
Chapter 30: Lower Smithfield Township, Northampton County, Pennsylvania..148
Chapter 31: March to Dupui's 152
Chapter 32: The Broadhead Rescue 156
Chapter 33: Back to Dupui's 161
Chapter 34: Christmas 1755 169
Chapter 35: Susquehanna Hunt 171
Chapter 36: Some Real Trouble 177
Chapter 37: Decisions 180
Chapter 38: Back Across the Fishkill 191
Chapter 39: What's to Be Done?...193

Afterword...200
About the Author 201
Bibliography 202
Additional Sources 203

Introduction

In 1719, Europeans had been living in North America for over a century but seldom more than a few miles inland from the Atlantic coastline. Eleven-year-old Solomon Davids, Jr. resided then, with his family, deep in a forest wilderness that would become known as the Minisink Valley. This wild land was also home to the Munsi Indians, who traded with Solomon's Father as they had with his father and his father before him. Times were sometimes hard but life was good.

Strangers arrived in the valley that summer. With them came rain. The outsiders plied their trade with curious tools and much debate. They made notes in journals. They discussed their findings, one with another, in hushed tones, while casting about suspicious looks. When these men left a month later, the valley was primed for change. The only question was how much and how soon.

Solomon Davids, Jr. grew to manhood during a time of transition. He experienced love and friendship, as his family struggled to survive in the harsh environment. He witnessed the collision of diverse cultures and personally felt the birth of both prejudice and hatred.

This is the account of rugged individuals, whose daily life choices were limited, far beyond their understanding, by geo-political decision-making a world away. In short, it is a true story of America.

Disclosure

This narrative is fiction based on historical fact. Most of the European characters were living people. The major events actually occurred. The places mentioned were authentic and located as near to the actual site as historical documentation could take me. I drew details from a journal kept, at the time, by John Reading, a surveyor from West New Jersey.[1]

Solomon Davids, Jr. was my great, great, great, great, great, great Grandfather. I descend from him through his daughter Belietje. I have endeavored here to be true to the spirit of their time and place, as I have the ability to know it. Obviously, the dialogue and some of the drama are fictionalized versions of a reality I can only read about and imagine.

---

[1] New Jersey at the time was separated officially into east and west halves.

Definitions

A few words and terms used in this text may not be in common use today, or may have a different meaning. To help the reader, I offer these few clarifications:

Bark	An early term used for a canoe built using birch-bark or elm-bark as the outer skin of the craft.
Dominie	A Dutch word from the time meaning minister or reverend.
Jaol	An early spelling for the word spelled today as jail.
Kill	A Dutch word used for creek or river. i.e. Fishkill, Paulinskill, Modderkill.
Machackemack	The present Neversink River.
Munsi	Delaware Indians / Leni Lenape.
Panther	North American Cougar.
Plantation	The word was used in the eighteenth century to refer to a farmstead. It was used in this area to refer to farmsteads both small and large. Later, the term seems to have taken on the connotation of today, which usually means a southern farm worked by slave labor. Although a few farmsteads in this area did have slaves, in the later years of this century, few people here owned slaves during the early years of settlement. The term is used, in this text, to refer only to a farmstead, because that was the word used most often in early documents.
Run	A term used at the time, to indicate a small stream or water flow. The term is noted on many old deeds from the era.

Spelling

In the eighteenth century, spelling did not seem to be of the greatest of importance to people. In records of the time, place and family names may be spelled differently in the same document, sometimes in the next paragraph, or maybe even the next sentence.

In this book, I was often forced to choose a specific spelling from multiple options. Thereafter, I attempt to be consistent in my own usage. However, in an effort to preserve authenticity, when I quote a source document, I do not attempt to "correct" their spelling or usage. As a result, family and place names may also be spelled differently in various locations of this text.

This may inadvertently cause the reader some confusion. I hope not too much.

Distances and Maps

What constitutes a long distance depends on whether you are walking, riding, or flying. Measuring distance in the seventeenth and eighteenth centuries was a great deal more challenging than it is today, when we benefit from satellites and global positioning devices. Still, it is amazing, sometimes, how close were the measurements of surveyors and cartographers of that time.

In this text, the distances noted for the local area usually were taken from the contemporary written documents. John Reading's Journal, in particular, gave several notations about the distances between locations in this community.

If no such information was available, I used the Google Earth measurement tool, which calculates (as the crows fly) in a direct line, rather than using road map measurements, which calculate as a pedestrian must, taking into account the difficulty of the terrain, and therefore traveling around obstacles like mountains and rivers.

In the text, I also provide a few maps for purposes of orientation and clarity. I do not consider myself a cartographer, by any stretch of the imagination, and beg the reader's indulgence and understanding for my sincere but crude efforts. These maps are not drawn to exact scale and cannot therefore be used to establish exact distances between the places noted. They should be used as intended; i.e. for general orientation and to clarify changes in land use or ownership over decades.

Acknowledgments

It is hard to understand history without considering the perspectives and prejudices of the people who write our books. The closest we get to truth is when we read source material, written or told of, by the actual participants or witnesses. Even here, facts are sometimes skewed by the opinions of the authors.

But thank god for letters, journals, diaries, baptismal records, land registrations, newspapers, and other original documents. Thanks also to all the people throughout the centuries who have protected and preserved them.

I would be remiss without mentioning and thanking specifically my friends at the:

Sussex County Historical Society; 82 Main St., Newton NJ

Minisink Valley Historical Society; 125-133 W. Main St. Port Jervis NY

Historical Society for Montague Township, Sussex County; 320 River Road, Montague NJ

Without the diligence and hard work of such people, much of our history would soon be lost. Without these particular individuals and groups, writing this book would have been far more difficult.

Special Thanks

**To my children,
Michelle, Michael, and Melissa,**
for their editorial comments and suggestions.
Brutal, though they sometimes were, their honest criticism
forced me to try harder.
I am so fortunate to have each of them in my life.

To David Harris,
for his candor, his belief in this story and my ability to tell it,
his dogged proofreading, his nagging imperative to find just
the right words, his steadfast encouragement and—most of
all—his enduring friendship.

To my brother, Larry,
for the art used on the cover of this book.

To my son-in-law, Roberto,
for his technical assistance and encouragement.

Dedication

This book is dedicated to my wife,

Brenda,

for her love, her support, and especially her patience,

without which, it could have never been written.

Preface

Two rarely blinking black eyes stare out from the cattail stalks. Suddenly, with a croak, the frog springs for the deep and disappears with a splash. Rings of water expand and shimmer in the moonlight, rolling over the reflective surface of the shallow pond.

The water settles. A small but powerful panther picks her way carefully along the top of a beaver dam, built of mud and sticks. She bounds off gracefully into the tall grass toward safety in the shadow of the trees. She moves tonight like the water flowing from the rocky dry ridges, westward through these highlands of small springs and beaver-dams, always down-slope, toward the flat land of large meadows and the river.

It is a good time for panthers. The summer rains are warm, and hunting is easy. There is yet little for a big cat to fear in this darkness.

Millions of acres of such country stretch away now, unbroken in every direction. The cat does not realize it, but, in this land of mountains and lakes, tall trees, and rocky outcrops, little has changed for thousands of years.

This is her range. It is everything she has known since she was a kit. All she will ever need or want is here.

But now, there are sometimes strange smells and different sounds in these forests. They are sounds and smells she has never experienced before. In the change she senses danger. She hunts with a new wariness. It is beyond her understanding, but it makes her nervous and fearful.

Storms at Kendiamong

Before the Munsi people were forced by the Iroquois to leave their ancestral home, they lived for centuries in the valleys of the Fishkill and Machackemack Rivers. The bark houses of the wolf clan were built on Great Minisink Island between the mountains of the Kittatinny, the Shawagunk, and the Pocono.

In those times, the Lenni Lenape--"the People"--lived in peace, hunting, fishing, and trading with their neighbors. White men had come to the upper part of their valley twenty-five summers before from white villages to the north on Rondout Creek. The Rondout flowed northeast into the big river called the Hudson. These settlers had asked permission, paying the Munsi for use of the land. The new neighbors had important items to trade. Copper kettles, steel awls, wool cloth, and black-powder muskets all made Indian life easier.

Beaver were still found then, not far to the west. Corn grew high in the fields. Shad still swam in the river. Game was plentiful. Life was good.

Our story begins in 1719, eighteen summers before the homeland of the Munsi changed forever.

Chapter 1: Morning in the Valley

It was that time of a June morning when eleven-year-old boys have rubbed the sleep from their eyes and filled their bellies full of cornmeal mush. A long, summer day stretched ahead, but the valley still lay, for the moment, in that last bit of darkness just before dawn.

This morning, a tawny panther sat poised on a bolder, overlooking a meadow of tall grass extending south and westward toward the Fishkill River. The grass lay quiet, and the cat watched for any sign of movement. A small cabin on the near side of the meadow appeared to her little more than a pile of logs. Suddenly, the cat's ears twitched forward as the muffled clunk of a wooden door latch reverberated across the distance.

A thick, plank door opened, and, for an instant, the panther could see into a human's den. Without complete understanding, the cat watched a stout woman silhouetted by a flickering fire. She stirred a cook-pot on the fire, which burned in a stone fireplace. A man sat behind a wooden table, sipping from a metal cup. The flame of a single candle in the middle of the table cast a dim circle of light. Suddenly, the view was obscured by a presence stepping through the doorway, and the plank door closed with a thump.

Eleven-year-old Solomon Davids, Jr. stepped his moccasined feet out onto the ground in front of the cabin. The boy paused. His eyes adjusted to the darkness. He could not see the cat watching him.

The morning air felt damp and heavy, but cool. Yesterday had been a scorcher. The call of a whip-poor-will greeted him from somewhere off toward the river. A mockingbird began its early morning song in the uplands to the east.

The boy smelled honeysuckle from the woods and the sweet scent of the pine resin, still seeping from the logs of the newly built cabin. He breathed in the essence of the morning and smiled.

Solomon was dressed in buckskin trousers and a linsey-woolsey shirt with a torn sleeve he had snagged on a thorn just the day before. A leather possible-bag rode on his left hip, hanging loose from a strap slung over his shoulder. He wore a leather belt with a sheath holding a bone-handled knife. In his right hand, he carried a five-foot-long hickory stick, which was about an inch in diameter. Using the sharp edge of his knife, the boy had meticulously shaved down any rough spots on the stick until it had at last felt comfortable and familiar in his hands. With these few things, Solomon was prepared to meet his day and whatever it might bring.

For a moment, the boy looked eastward toward the mountain. Today, the hulking ridgeline stood black against a grey-blue sky, that sky growing bluer with each passing moment. Puffs of dark grey cloud floated above. But those clouds would soon transform to white, as the sun lit this morning. It looked and smelled to Solomon as if it would be a clear, warm day. Drawing in a short breath, he trotted off along the dirt road, assuming the steady, bouncy pace of an old fox out for a long hunt.

As the boy headed south, the panther turned, padding quietly into the trees. Before long, more humans would be about their business in the flatlands. Instinctively, the cat knew she would be safer during daylight in the rocky crags of the high country.

Soon the sun peaked over the Kittatinny Ridge, and Solomon trotted from the road onto a downhill path following a small run. His Pa called this creek the Modderkill. It was a rocky little run, no more than a dozen feet across. Flowing out of mountain springs to the east, it meandered its way from here toward the river.

The boy stopped as he moved into the grassland, not because he needed rest, but to listen and learn what could be learned. The sounds were the same as he had heard from the cabin, except that, from here, the mockingbird seemed now a little farther off and the whip-poor-will seemed a bit closer. Other creatures were joining the morning song. The loud hammering of a woodpecker caught his ear, and he thought aloud, "far off... maybe across the river."

Resuming his easy pace, he continued along the narrow track. The tall grass transitioned here to shorter bunch grass. Here and there grew a scattering of wild-strawberry vine and gooseberry bushes heavy this time of year with their ripening fruit. Not far ahead, he recognized familiar giant cottonwoods, as he moved steadily toward the river.

Stopping yet again, Solomon listened once more to the awakening of the day. He loved the sounds of morning in the valley. There was always something to hear or see if only a person listened or watched long enough. Today all seemed well in his valley, so on he trotted, breathing easily and enjoying the morning as only a boy his age ever can.

Chapter 2: The War Cry

By the time the panther reached her lair, hidden among the tall bracken-ferns and big rocks of the Kittatinny Ridges, the sun was two hours high. At the river, Solomon bent over the water's edge and strung his tenth sunfish onto a braided horsehair stringer. He tossed the fish on the stringer back into the clear water.

He looked up, his eyes now scanning the mouth of the Modderkill, where it emptied out into the wide waters of the Fishkill. In the big river, wind-tossed ripples glinted in the sunlight, and the faint scent of wood smoke came wafting upstream to greet him.

Solomon watched southward, hoping to see a bark canoe round the bend carrying two Indian boys his way, their paddles flashing in the sunlight. Instead, he saw two braves glide quickly along in a large dugout floating downstream toward the village.

He was tired of fishing. He thought maybe his friends would not come today. Someone else may have needed their canoe, or possibly they had decided to go up the Raymondskill to fish for trout.

Across the river near the far bank, Solomon suddenly noticed a long-legged, slate blue bird standing in the water. He had, at first, mistaken the bird for a small stump. Now, he was fascinated by its stillness.

He watched the bird for a few minutes to see if it might strike. It did not. He was not close enough to see if its eyes ever blinked, but he knew what he was watching. It was a bird patiently awaiting its prey.

"If I wait as the heron does," he thought, "my friends may yet be along."

For a short while, Solomon busied himself listening to the noise of some distant crows, but the birds were so far away he could hardly tell their direction. He was bored. The breeze freshened, rustling the leaves around him. Suddenly, he was hungry. Remembering the gooseberries, he trotted up the trail through the shade of the tall trees, back the way he had come.

In a few minutes, Solomon was popping tiny berries into his mouth, one after another, for a tart summer taste. Under his shirt, he could feel sweat beginning to trickle down his back.

"It's getting hot out here in the open sun," he thought.

The sharp cry of a wren interrupted the boy's thoughts. But, something was different. This was not the normal sweet song of the small bird. It was instead an impassioned cry, designed to attract the attention of the gods or anyone else who might be listening.

He spotted the angry little creature a few paces to his left, frantically flitting from limb to limb on a gooseberry bush, causing quite a commotion.

"What's his problem?" the boy wondered.

With sure-footed and watchful steps, Solomon stalked slowly forward to investigate. Then, suddenly, he froze in place, with an uplifted foot, as he had seen deer often do just before an arrow was let fly. Barely a yard away, stretched out in the grass, lay a rattlesnake.

Carefully and deliberately, Solomon pulled back his raised foot, placing it again to the ground, never for an instant relinquishing his balance. Watching those dirty brown and yellow bands lurking there in the grass, the boy's eyes narrowed, his jaw tightened, and his entire countenance seemed to harden. Solomon hated rattlesnakes.

He had his reasons. Only two years before, a warm, new puppy had nipped at his fingers and licked his face. That plump, black-and-tan bundle of fur had waddled about the cabin in the late weeks of that winter, sniffing out much mischief and scampering away at the first sign of danger.

The dog learned quickly to nuzzle the boy's leg when he wanted attention. And attention was the one thing he seemed to crave above all else. Soon, the dog had trained the boy though the lad thought it was the other way round. The little hound especially enjoyed having his master scratch the soft spot just under his chin.

All this pleased not only the dog, but also the boy. Both took special delight in having their very own companion who always appreciated everything the other did, even if it might be wrong or awkwardly done. Quickly the two became inseparable.

Day after day the boy and the dog tramped the woods until they were so weary they could hardly drag themselves back to the cabin before dark. On cool mornings, the little hound always found a good place to curl up and sleep in the warmth of the sun, so Solomon named his pup Sun-dog.

Then last summer, when he and Sun-dog were roaming the woods not far from the cabin. Solomon heard a rattle. He recognized the sound, and froze in his fear.

Solomon saw Sun-dog move forward and he cried "wait!" But it was too late. The snake struck. The dog was bitten. He died the next day—a slow and painful death—the boy holding him tenderly and sobbing more with each of the dog's last, tortured breaths.

Before the death of Sun-dog, Solomon had not hated snakes. The boy had been taught that snakes were a natural part of his world. He had learned of the rattlesnake's dangerous, poisonous venom. But he also learned that even rattlers struck rarely, except to eat or when they felt threatened. He knew the rattle was a warning. He believed then what the Munsi storytellers taught: snakes were part of the Great Spirit's plan for this valley. But he had never exactly understood why.

After Sun-dog was killed, Solomon just didn't care about any of that. He felt shame because of his fear. He remembered the helplessness and the grief. He believed he was responsible, somehow, for the dog's death.

He missed Sun-dog terribly. He grew angrier and angrier. Then, one day, as he sat quietly eating his cornmeal mush, he simply decided.

"I *hate* rattlesnakes! I'll kill every one I see, for as long as I live."

Now one of the dangerous foes lay before him. The boy saw that the snake held a small wren in its expanding jaws, the bird's eyes already glazed in the shock of its pending death. There was no way the wren could be saved.

But Solomon's sworn enemy was vulnerable now, too. The rattler could not rid itself of its prey. It must wait to swallow.

Without hesitation, Solomon leaped forward with his stick, clubbing the head of the snake, feathers and blood splattering in all directions. The boy jumped back.

Re-gripping his weapon, he sprang again at the snake. Jabbing furiously with the blunt end of the stick, he repeatedly bashed the snake's head until the cold beady eyes with the expanding jaw and the little bird were one bloody mess of smashed skin, broken bones, and scattered feathers.

Then, carefully using the stick, Solomon pinned what was left of the snake's head to the ground. As the thick, menacing tail writhed slowly back and forth, Solomon pulled his knife from its sheath and, with a single accurate swipe, severed the snake's head. Then, with the stick, he tossed the snake body into a nearby bush to finish its death dance.

Instinctively, the boy screamed. The loud, clear sound rang out boldly across the meadow, echoing back in waves from the surrounding forest, announcing to the world: "I'm here! I've killed my enemy! And I am still alive!"

In the instant of silence, which followed, from high above the grassland, a red-tailed hawk answered the boy's cry with a predatory scream of its own.

Chapter 3: The Strangers

The panther, lying concealed among the high country ferns, did not hear Solomon's war-whoop, but she heard the hawk reply. Near the river, the boy stood among the gooseberry bushes trembling from the excitement of his battle.

He had killed before, but never like this. At other times, having stalked his prey, there was a moment after the deed was done, when he felt differently. As he had been taught, he usually offered a prayer for the spirit of the creatures he killed.

But this time there was no regret. He felt instead a primitive pride and strength at his control over life and death. For the first time, Solomon was experiencing the taste of revenge. For him, on this day, the flavor was particularly sweet.

Solomon did not concern himself that this rattlesnake was likely not the one that killed his dog. Looking for the exact one would be like looking for one particular pebble in the river or one specific acorn in the forest. It was enough, for him, that this creature belonged to the same tribe. He intended never to hesitate and never to show mercy. Today, Solomon remembered Sun-dog. For Sun-dog—for the loss of his friend—Solomon meant to make every rattlesnake pay. This was just the first one of many he intended to kill.

It was over for now, but his heart still pounded rapidly in his chest. He walked proudly over to watch the headless carcass writhe, slowly, without purpose, in the bush. Laying his weapon aside, he reached into his possible-bag, pulling out a short, leather string. Using his knife, he quickly gutted the creature, and, with the string, he tied what was left of his enemy securely to his belt. He would skin the snake later and nail the hide on the barn to dry. The rattles, he thought, would make a fine trophy memorializing his success in this battle, the first in what he intended to be a lifetime campaign to make his world safe from rattlesnakes.

He drew in a long, deep breath. He squinted his eyes and slowly scanned out across the meadow. Red-winged black birds were flitting among the willows near the river and resuming their song. A light breeze rustled the tall reed-grasses. Solomon picked up his stick and stood listening again to the sounds of his world. Then, the boy turned and quickly trotted back to the Fishkill. He found his willow fishing pole still stuck in the mud where he had left it.

Gazing downriver, the boy saw no signs of a canoe. Looking across the river, he saw that the heron now, too, was gone. He shrugged his shoulders.

Solomon bent down to inspect his stringer full of fish. They were all secure, but he noticed the ones strung early this morning did look a bit sluggish now. Dropping them back into the water, he rose, wondering what he should do next.

He was startled, suddenly, seeing the stranger standing across the stream only a few yards away. Where had he come from?

The man was dressed much like Solomon—leather breeches, homespun shirt, moccasins, possible-bag slung over the shoulder, knife in a leather sheath. But the stranger held a heavy musket by its barrel with the stock casually at rest over his shoulder. The man looked sun-browned and some worn. But he seemed well fed and possessed a muscular athletic build. He appeared to be at home in the backcountry. He was smiling. He was not the one who had just been taken unaware.

Few white men ever came to the valley through the mountains from the south. "Maybe a trader like Pa" thought Solomon. But something about the man didn't look right for a trader or farmer or blacksmith.

Solomon noticed then a second figure, picking his way through the rocks toward them but yet some fifty yards distant. The second man led a small, spotted horse along the river path. Beyond the man with the horse, laurel thicket screened the view, but off in that direction Solomon heard another horse blow and then noticed the understory trees beyond swaying apart and springing back together. Other men and horses were straggling this way.

"They must be heavily packed," he thought, "making it a tight squeeze on that fishermen's' path". How many and who are they, he wondered. Why are they here?

He did not like being surprised in his home country. But what was to be done now? The newcomer saw the boy's predicament and stood where he was. With a smile, he asked, "is this the way to the house of Solomon Davids?"

The boy hesitated, and then, realizing the man was asking about his father, he answered in the steadiest voice he could muster, "that trail to the road, then north."

He pointed to the well-worn pathway on the stranger's side of the creek. Solomon knew, that here, that trail cut away from the river to the east-south-east toward a gap through the mountains. It would be three-quarters of a mile before it crossed the only pathway within two hundred miles, which anyone could fairly call a road. He thought to himself that the faint game trail at his back would get him to the cabin well before these men arrived. But he must get rid of them now so he could alert Pa to the presence of outsiders in the valley.

The stranger turned, taking a few paces toward his advancing companion and emitting a shrill whistle. His friend looked up and the stranger waved his arm in a slow motion, pointing in the direction of the road.

The man with the musket turned back toward the Modderkill. The fishing pole was still stuck in the mud, fish still swirled on the stringer; but the boy with the snake was gone.

The traveler smiled, turning down the path leading toward the road.

Chapter 4: The News

With the foreigners behind him, Solomon still ran toward the cabin fifteen minutes after leaving the river. There had been no time to pause or catch his breath. He couldn't remember ever running this hard. As he sped along, his moccasined feet throbbing on the dusty summer trail, he wondered what his Pa would say about these strangers.

His air was coming in short deep pulls now, his muscles ached, sweat streamed down his face. As he approached the cabin he was pleased to see a gray horse and two sorrels hobbled and grazing in the meadow. Between breaths, he shouted "Pa" as he sprinted up, his legs burning from the effort.

Solomon Davids Sr. emerged from the door of his barn just as his son collapsed gratefully and exhausted into his arms. Gasping for breath, the boy spilled out all his news in a jumbled rush, between the gulps for more air.

Amazingly his father seemed neither concerned nor surprised. "Sorry boy," he said.

"Jacob and Three-tongues already beat you here with the news, although I guess you are the first to actually see any of this bunch in the valley. We've been told to expect 'em. They're surveyors. From the Jerseys and Pennsylvania too, I reckon."

Solomon Sr. gazed up the dirt road toward the north.

"Some others are already at Westfalls'. Came from Goshen. The ones fer New York are comin' down the road to Swartworts' up at Peenpack, though nobody has seen sign of 'em yet. The ones you saw must have come through the Water Gap. They're goin' to stay with Decker".

By the time all this was said, Solomon's Ma was ringing the bell hanging beside the cabin door. It was a small, iron bell, manufactured in Amsterdam. It had been passed down in Ma's family from her great-grandfathers time, but it rang loud enough to be heard through the fields and buildings surrounding the farm. Mrs. Davids was a middle-aged woman, already gray headed from the life of a frontier wife and mother. She knew how to gather her family.

Soon, the entire Davids brood was in front of their cabin, along with Jake Kuckendal and Three-tongues, who where in the trading business with Pa, but kinda like family too. Together they milled about, kicking dirt and watching the road from the south, as it stretched out across the meadow.

Five-year-old Jan[2] ran across the road and scampered up the nearest young apple tree, like a hungry squirrel climbing up an oak. Soon, he was high enough to make the small limbs sway, and his Ma yelled to him, in her no-nonsense tone, "be careful not to break those limbs!"

Ma's trees were already heavy with their summer crop. They were not quite ready for picking, but, in her mind, she had every apple from her young orchard counted and preserved.

"I see 'em," Jan yelled. "One, two, three, four, five, six!"

It was well that there were no more riders because Jan had reached his limit in sums. Deliberately the horsemen came on, their horses at a slow plodding walk, and Ma said,

"There are seven horses, Johnny. The last man has a pack animal".

With her comment she looked at Solomon Jr. and asked, "where'd you get that snake?"

Solomon had almost forgotten he was wearing his first ever battle trophy. Now all eyes were suddenly on him.

"Down by the river," he answered.

"Those snakes will kill you, boy!" Ma replied.

---

[2] Jan= Dutch spelling of John.

Her comment brought a smile to every face in the small crowd. Belietje Davids probably said that something or another was going to kill someone in the family almost every day. It seemed to be her job to worry. She tried to anticipate every danger and point them out to her offspring—she was good at it, too.

She was usually right. But, unfortunately, hereabouts there were so many things that could kill you, her comment had become sort of a joke within the family. She saw the smiles now, but she did not share the humor. She frowned and said, "Well, go skin it and bring me the meat! We'll need to add it to the turnips and summer-greens I've got cookin'. Looks like we're havin' company."

A few moments later the strangers rode up to the cabin. It was a hot day. The horses were lathered and shining-slick with sweat. Occasionally one of the weary animals would shudder, toss a head, or flick a tail in their eternal summer struggle to keep off biting flies and swarming gnats.

The lead horse stopped in front of the cabin with no apparent direction from his rider. All the horses, then, seemed to halt at once, drop their heads, and begin to sniff the ground. Soon the horses shifted their weight to rest on three legs but none of the riders had taken the energy to dismount just yet. The men looked haggard, but fit. It was clear this was not the first long ride for any of them.

"Good to see you, John," he heard his father say. "You too, Tom." He added, "How you boys been?"

Then, turning to Jake, Pa said, "This is John Reading and Tom Wetherill."

Reading spoke up. "We just came through the gap and it weren't as easy as you said Sol—leastwise not fer us. The skeeters were the size of birds and the gnats almost as big. But we got through, just as you said we would."

He rose up in the saddle to stretch his back muscles, which seemed to squeak and groan along with the saddle leather.

"It wasn't too bad coming up the far side of the big hill, but comin' down this side was a bit scary. The pack animal took quite a little fall, head over hooves, down a 30-foot drop. Thought she was killed sure. But when we got down to her, she got right up and shook it off. We only broke a bottle of lime juice in the whole deal."

Then he turned, nodding successively toward each of the other men as he introduced them to Solomon and his family, "This is Joseph Kirkbride and that is James Steel. That big feller there is Jacob Taylor and that's John Chapman. Tom you already know."

Reading leaned out away from his horse, cleared the dust from his throat and spat on the ground. Then he said, "Boys this is Solomon Davids the trader we told you about. He's the originator of the little map that got us here. If you didn't like the trip, he's the man to blame. He knows this area as well as any white man I recon. Tom and I shared many a fire with this gentleman when he was trading over on the Raritan a few years back."

He smiled, looking down at Solomon Sr. and said, "He's a man you can trust. And he usually has good brandy too. Is this the misses Sol?"

"This is my wife, Belietje. That's Jacob Kuckendal, my partner. This is my good friend, Three-tongues. The boys are Jorris, Solomon Jr., and Jan."

Then Solomon Sr. asked, "How's your father, John? I'm surprised he isn't along."[3]

"Father died last spring of the fever," the man replied.

Solomon Jr. had never known the dead man they spoke of, but his Pa seemed saddened by the news.

"Sorry to hear it," he said, looking down at the ground.

---

[3] John Reading's father, of the same name, was also a surveyor. Both he and his son lived on the Raritan River in West New Jersey, further south and east of the Minisink Valley.

For a moment the conversation paused. But then the man named Kirkbride said, "Wouldn't your old man have loved this adventure!" And the men all laughed, and nodded in agreement.

The boy watched all this from beside the left front corner of the cabin where he was skinning the snake. The third rider in line, the man called Tom, was the stranger he had spoken with at the Modderkill. When their eyes met, Tom Wetherill smiled again and quietly saluted his new acquaintance by touching his right hand to his hat.

The boy, who was carefully peeling off the last of the snake hide, nodded in response. Next he cut the hide free of the rattles, which were hanging limp at the tip of the tail. Then with his knife he deftly sliced the rattles from the snake body, catching them in his left hand, and reaching up, he placed them between the cabin logs as high as he could reach, under the eaves, back against the chinking, where they would dry. Finally he took the carcass from the skinning spike and, as the riders began dismounting, he carried the meat inside.

Chapter 5: Supper

Two hours after the strangers rode in, the turnips and greens from the garden were eaten. So too were two roasted rabbits, the fried snake, and a good deal of dried venison and some smoked shad. A jug from the springhouse had appeared, making its rounds among the men until it too was almost empty.

While the visitors enjoyed their leisure Solomon Jr. and his older brother Jorris watered their horses at the wooden water trough below the spring house, careful not to let any horse drink too much. Then they brought the animals back into the meadow where they hobbled, unsaddled and unbridled the riding horses, brushing each animal lightly as they had been taught. They then turned them loose to amble off toward the tall, luscious grass waiting in the meadow.

The pack animal remained saddled but her most burdensome pack was removed by John Chapman, who came out to care for her. He was a strong, square-jawed young, man who didn't talk much. He tethered the packhorse on a thirty-foot rope with a long metal pin driven into the ground. Then he poured a small measure of oats into a nose-bag and slipped it over her head. The other horses smelled the grain and sauntered over, but they got none. When she finished eating the oats, Chapman took the bag off and stored it in one of the packs, returning to the cabin, without ever speaking to the boys.

Soon the riding horses were grazing or rolling in the tall grass and the boys slipped into the cabin to listen. Most of the food had been finished. The pipes were lit, and a haze of blue tobacco smoke hung heavy in the air. Reading was speaking.

"The Board of Property down in Philadelphia have sent along Steel and Taylor here, as kinda unofficial members of the expedition, to represent them and report back on our findings. The real question right now is between the two Jerseys and New York, but I guess Pennsylvania has a stake. At least they think they do, don't they James?"

James Steel did not speak. But he nodded his head in reply, taking a long drag on his pipe, and exhaling the smoke, in contemplative little round circles, which floated slowly toward the roof, before disappearing.

Reading noted his response with an understanding grunt and droned on with his own story of their journey and why they all were here.

Another half hour passed, before Joseph Kirkbride finally interrupted Reading's dissertation.

"John, if we're to see Decker's place before dark, shouldn't we be getting along?"

Reading pause, and then smiled with a good-natured nod, "Joseph, you're right, as usual, let's get there."

"Thank you ma'am, for a fine meal, it was much needed," he said rising from his chair and stepping quickly toward the door. The others suddenly hustled along to follow him outside.

Briskly the strangers retrieved their horses and began to saddle up. Soon the survey expedition was repacked and mounted, with most trotting off, north, along the old road, heading for the John Decker homestead.

After mounting and settling himself in the saddle, John Reading looked back down at the family.

"We'll be back fer another drink in a few days, Solomon. We still got some catching up to do."

He smiled, tipping his hat to Ma who stood in the doorway listening to every word with a tired sweat-stained face. Guests were a rare blessing in her world.

"Ma'am, when we call again, could you get that boy to kill another snake to go with the fixin's? It was mighty tasty."

Ma waved her hand, flashing a quick smile, and turned back inside.

Solomon Jr. had not been offered the jug when it passed, but his head was swirling now with the excitement of his day. Strange and wondrous things were happening in his valley. Solomon had never heard so much news from the settlements before, and certainly not from so many different sources.

When news had come in the past it was from a solitary trader or two. They always carried stories but seemed more interested in answers to questions. Rivers, trails and mountain passes were their main interests. Not that these new men didn't ask many of those same questions. But the new strangers were different. They were well informed about the latest business of the Proprietors in Elizabethtown and Philadelphia, and the Royal Governor in far away Albany.

News from the settlements was always exciting. Farmers from Machackemack or Peenpack occasionally went to Esopus for supplies, or to get married in the church, have a baby christened or on other important business. Upon their return they always politely made the rounds to every cabin in the valley. Bringing back the news was important.

Occasionally there was a party. Often times at these parties, letters were read aloud, for folks who themselves could not decipher written words on paper. But never before had important men come to the valley in groups, like this. These men were here on the King's business.

"God save the King," Solomon thought, as he had heard others often say.

More surveyors were being sent by the Royal Governor of New York, if they had not already arrived. There would be meetings and discussions and maybe a bit of showmanship he heard his father comment. But he had also heard Pa whisper anxiously to Jake, "this is going to be mighty important."

As the strangers rode out of sight, Solomon Jr. heard a low rumble from the west. Glancing toward the Fishkill he saw dark, summer, storm clouds, forming over the Poconos.

Chapter 6: The Farm

It rained during the night. Solomon awoke next morning to the gentle patter, then steady rattle, then loud rumble of raindrops falling on the oak shakes above his head, and the not so hushed sounds of his father's grumbling in the cabin below.

"We don't need this rain. We need sun! And heat! To bring along the wheat and dry the hay."

Solomon Sr. was an Indian trader, but also a farmer. More than that, he was now a land owner and speculator. He had paid the Munsi years past, in trade goods, for his farm. Then, a little over a year ago, he paid the East Jersey Proprietors for the right to own the land, by getting a half interest in a patent on one thousand acres. A surveyor named Thomas Stevens had determined, that the New Jersey Proprietors had the King's right of possession, to this particular land in the valley. So Pa and this new partner, Stevens, were now the 'official' landowners.

"To profit, this land must attract farmers willing to buy," he heard his father say.

"This farm is the first working place on the patent. We must show it will grow crops well enough to support families this far out on the frontier. "

Solomon Jr. raised his head, sniffing the air. "Biscuits," he thought. "They sure smell good."

It was a cozy morning to be snug in a warm, dry bed. The boy listened to his pa speaking, now in quieter tones, to his ma:

"Our flax will yield well. The corn is knee high with a strong root this year. It will soon need the hoe again but I'm hopeful. All four of our sheep are strong and healthy. The cow gives almost two gallon of milk and the horse is sound. With some profits from the tradin' we may be able to buy that brace of oxen this fall."

"That would be good," he heard his mother reply, but her voice sounded unconvinced.

"Your orchard is just beginning to come into its prime," his father went on as if he hadn't heard her.

"The pumpkin and squash are as big as any grown by the Munsi women. The soil here is as black and rich as any I've seen. I may not be the best farmer in the valley, but even I can make a paying plantation of this place. The boys are good help now. By-golly we could get rich sellin' this land."

"That would be good," said Ma.

But, before this business of actually selling the land could get started, there were questions that had to be answered. This was a long way from the settlements; things were always unpredictable here.

Only twenty-five years earlier the first white man had been invited to settle here by the Indians themselves. He was a blacksmith named Tietsort who had built a cabin in the upper part of the valley on Machackemack Branch.

Before coming here, Tietsort had lived with his family in Schenectady, twelve miles north of Albany. In 1689, the French and their allies, the Huron, had surprised everyone with a winter nighttime raid, burning the little village to the ground, killing or dragging away the inhabitants.

Tietsort, a young man then, escaped into the darkness, arriving bloodied and exhausted in Albany next morning, to sound the alarm. He was one of few who survived. Solomon Sr.'s own uncle, Christofellson Davids, with his wife and four children were burned up in their cabin that terrible night.

It had all happened long before Solomon Jr. had been born. But his father sometimes told the story if anyone mentioned Frenchmen or French Indians. Solomon Sr. hated anything French, and the story always ended with the same conclusion.

"The Huron and the French are not like us, they're more like Bob-cat who start raiding your trap line. You can't reason with 'em; you just have to kill 'em."

After a while, Mr. Tietsort the blacksmith had found a productive life again, living here among the peaceful Munsi people. In return the local Indians benefitted from his considerable skills at the forge.

Over the years other white families like the Gumars, Swartwoods, and Wesfalias had followed, negotiating and paying the Indians for the use of the land. But Machackemack Branch was a long way from the nearest Christian settlements. Kingston was sixty miles north, a three-day trip by horseback. The Man-Hattens were eighty miles east-southeast through difficult highlands. Most families saw little reason to move that far, into the wilderness, to live among the savages. So the Valley settlement had remained small.

The Decker and Davids families, along with a few others, had come in more recent times. Solomon's father and grandfather had conducted trade, with the Munsi, for many years before moving here. Indeed, Solomon's Great-grandfather Christoffel[4] had traded with the Munsi from his cabin on Rondout Creek, decades before.

Presently, there were some 25 families living from the upper community at Peenpack down along the Machackemack River, to its mouth at the Fishkill. From the Blacksmith's place south, people called it the lower community, but from John Decker's farm south, there were no other white plantations except the Davids cabin, at the lowland meadows called Kendiamong.

In the Fishkill River, three miles south of the Davids Place, lay Great Minisink Island, home to the Wolf Clan of the Munsi Tribe. The Munsi, would later be known as the

---

[4] Chrisoffel Davids appears often in the early Dutch Court Records at Fort Orange. He was an Indian trader and interpreter with a colorful and somewhat violent history. He lived in a cabin on Rondout creek south of Esopus (Later called Kingston after the English/Dutch war).

Delaware Indian Nation. The Munsi themselves had been driven here, from their temperate southern highlands by their Cherokee enemies a couple centuries before Tietsort.

But here, even the Munsi did not exactly live free. The powerful and warlike Iroquois Confederation, residing further north, extracted annual tribute payments from the Munsi for the privilege of living under their protective covenant.

Now, without consulting or informing the Munsi, here were representatives of these colonial governments, arriving to decide among themselves what parts of this land the King of England had granted to each of them.

The Dutch had discovered and claimed this area for over half a century, before surrendering control of it to the English in 1664. The French continued to push their claims south and east from their stronghold in New France. New France made claims to lands so far west, only the king's cartographers ever thought much about them. These claims like the Frenchmen themselves followed the rivers of the interior which, it was said, flowed all the way from New France in the North Country to the southern gulf where the French were busy building new towns and ports which people said would remain free from ice even in winter. This, if it were to continue and become consolidated, might ruin the lucrative fur trade now enjoyed by many folks in these English colonies. It was a serious and growing concern.

There seemed to be so much wilderness, but yet, never quite enough to satisfy every-ones needs for more land, more furs, and easier routes to the trading.

Solomon Jr. had heard the stories of his valley's settlement, while sitting around the fireside, listening to his Ma, Pa, Jake Kuckendal and other neighbors, chatting away cold winter nights. But, he remembered when the surveyor Mr. Stevens arrived in the valley.

Thomas Stevens had come only a couple summers ago, with a crew of three hired men and all kinds of strange equipment. They used metal chain to measure from the river, across the lowlands, to the ridges beyond. Solomon Jr. understood now, what surveys were about. He knew his Pa and others wanted to be sure no one could officially take from them, the land they had settled, bought and paid for.

Mr. Stevens had been one of the first surveyors from New Jersey to ever visit this valley. Most of the farms northward, if they had, a written title, were in the upper community, where New York had issued a few vaguely described patents.

Solomon Jr. had heard Stevens explain that the boundary between these colonies, would depend upon the location of a point, on the upper most branch of the River Delaware, where it crossed latitude forty-one degrees and forty minutes. The trouble was, no one in the colonies knew where that point lie. No one was even sure which branch was the most northern of the Delaware.

The boy was astonished, when he suddenly understood, that the Delaware River Stevens kept talking about was the river he knew as the Fishkill. His very own fishing hole might be the point they were seeking.

But Solomon Jr. had heard Stevens tell his Pa, "the point they're looking for is certainly much farther to the north. Our patent in East Jersey should be plenty safe."

Now, these new men were here in the valley to determine the placement of that station point. Solomon Jr. sensed tension in his father's comment to Jake. He remembered Pa saying often "when the 'Gentlemen' and 'Lawyers' get hold of a thing, day often turns to night and night to day". So, as he lay listening to the growing drum of rain on the shingles above, he wondered, what would be the result of all the attention to this valley—the valley he and his Munsi neighbors called home?

24

Delaware River

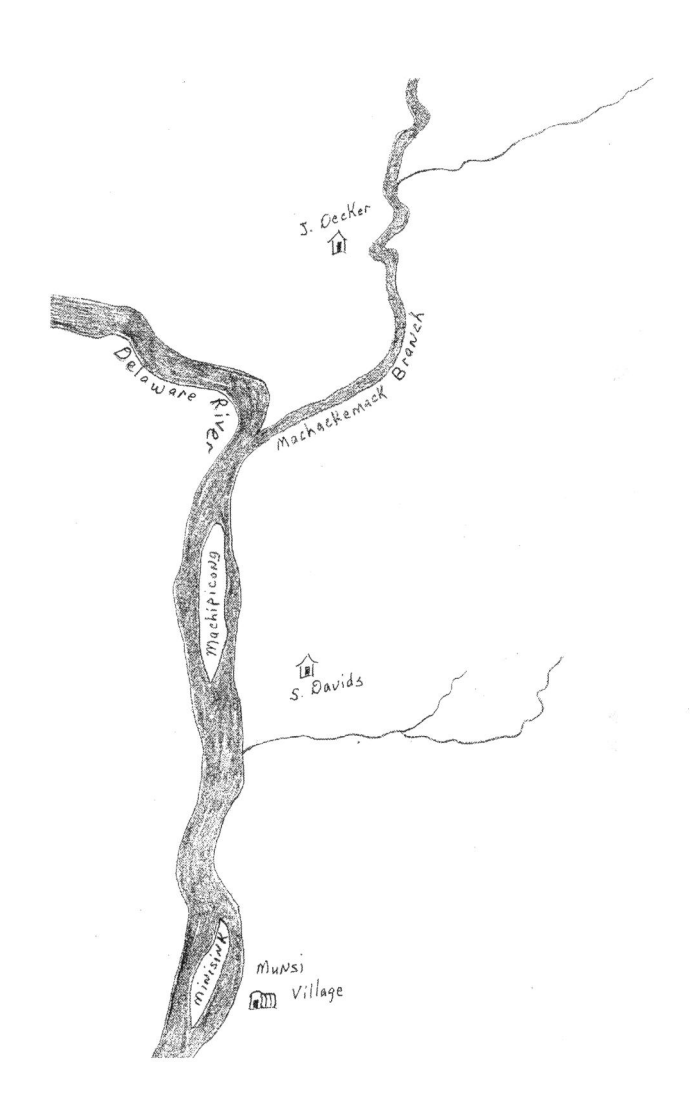

J. Oecker

Machackemack Branch

Machipicong

S. Davids

Minisink

Munsi Village

Chapter 7: The Mission

*T*hree days after killing the rattlesnake, Solomon Jr. returned home from the river, where he and his Munsi friends Twisted-stalk and Red-corn had been fishing. It had been a poor day of fishing. A black horse and a sorrel, with one rear white stocking, were hobbled with his father's big grey gelding in the meadow.

Inside the cabin Solomon could hear voices. As he drew open the door the boy found Thomas Wetherill and a new man sitting at the table with his Pa, Jake, and yet another jug from the springhouse. Ma was busily tending an iron kettle on the hearth. Jorris, Three-tongues, and Jan were still about somewhere outside. Solomon plopped down on a three-legged stool to listen.

"Tom, I told you before, there ain't no other main branch between here and the Susquehanna," he heard his father say.

"I know you did Sol, and we all know you're telling us straight, but the dang Yorkers have got to be convinced. We did some observations before we left Decker's and concluded the latitude is north sixteen or seventeen more miles. As you very well know, the Fishkill is winding far off to the west. There's no tellin' how far we'll have to go to set that point.

Decker says its rough piney country. Meantime they want a guide to take a man all the way to the Susquehanna, just to be sure we're right, when we get the station fixed on this branch. It will pay good money, and you said yourself, it wouldn't take mor'n a week or two."

Tom went on explaining that there were now fourteen commissioners and surveyors officially assigned to the expedition. They were representing each of the four Colonial interests and they came along with six more men on wages and a couple of slaves. It was a big undertaking.

"No one person," he said, "is clearly in charge of the whole shebang. So far all they have done is talk a lot, determined where the point is not and argue."

He chuckled more to himself than the others and then said, "But Reading and our crew did catch a few good sunfish t'other evening".

He laughed along with the others and Ma interrupted slapping two wooden trenchers filled with beans and summer greens onto the table. Wetherill's crony had said hardly a word but went right to work without hesitation on Ma's cooking.

After supper Pa pushed his chair back from the table and reached for his pipe. He looked earnestly at Wetherill and said, "Now tell me about this feller they've picked to go along to the Susquehanna".

Solomon Jr. soon forgot about his poor day of fishing.

The conversation ebbed and flowed. When the talk was over Jacob and Three-tongues agreed to guide the Expedition's chosen man to the Susquehanna River Valley. Next morning, June 28th, 1719, the two guides, along with Wetherill and his stoic companion, left on horseback, heading for Decker's farm.

Chapter 8: The River

Jorris lowered the bark canoe to the water. The sliver of a moon hung in a clear sky over the Kittatinny's. To the west a purple hue still clung to the crests of the Poconos. The smell of fresh-water mussel shells, engulfed them in the twilight, and a raccoon squealed suddenly from somewhere upriver.

Solomon tossed in two waxed grey canvas bags, each stuffed with a wool blanket. He handed Jorris a paddle keeping the other for himself. His brother held the craft by the gunnels and Solomon crawled into the bow assuming his paddling position.

As soon as his butt rested on his heels, mosquitoes began buzzing his ear and biting the soft skin of his neck. The boy paid them no mind. He had applied the bear grease. There wasn't much else that could be done but endure them till first frost. The buzzing, little bloodsuckers were just part of summer here in the valley.

Jorris pushed the little bark out into the river. As it glided forward he slipped cat-like over the stern into the craft. With a few strokes the boys maneuvered their canoe out into the current. The little bark, beginning to pick up speed, left some of the mosquitoes behind.

"Mosquitoes are always fewer out in the big water," thought Solomon as he paused his paddle and readjusted his position. "More wind and less to eat I suppose."

The little craft continued forward without a sound now, save the quiet ripple of the bow cutting the surface.

Nothing was said. Nothing needed to be said. The boys knew this river well, from here to Minisink. Tonight there was adequate water to float the shoals waiting around the next bend. From that point south, there was always enough to float a canoe. The swift water would make a quick trip. Tomorrow's trip, coming back upstream, would be the hard part.

Solomon felt secure with his brother in the stern. Jorris was thirteen. He was experienced on the river and a steady hand at the helm. He could handle a canoe as well as the Munsi and better than most whites. The boys liked being on the river.

Jorris had built this little bark himself last summer, with the help of Twisted-stalk and his father Half-moon. It had been a tedious task. But he had performed skillfully and with pride. Every last seam was well sealed with pine-pitch. There were no leaks.

As they rounded the bend something large and alive moved now, through the water, in the shadows near the eastern shore. Jorris finished his stroke, letting his paddle slide out behind. Skillfully turning the blade, he steered his craft to the right, as the shadowy presence froze in its place. Solomon paused his stroke again, and both boys held their breath, trying not to move.

When they were directly astern, the bear grunted "rrrooofff!" and splashed ashore with a great commotion. The brothers in the canoe glided safely past about ten yards further out in the stream. Moonlight caught the glint of a smile, as Solomon glanced over his shoulder at his brother.

"Seeing the bear is a good sign," he thought.

Silently he dipped his paddle back into the big river.

◈

Soon, the brothers passed Solomon's fishing hole at the mouth of the Modderkill and a few minutes later Jorris steered the canoe into the left branch of the river at the head of Great Minisink Island. The island is a mile and half long. The eastern branch, known locally as the Benakill, is the shorter, faster route. The other branch makes a long, slow, bend around the west side of the island.

Floating the Benakill, the boys began to hear the rasping sound of heavy leaves being blown together in a fresh breeze. The smell of turned earth, beans, corn, squash, and pumpkin, growing on the island in large fields, permeated the night air. A dog barked, off in the distance.

Smells of wood-smoke and roasting venison grew stronger as they drifted south, and Solomon's mouth began to water.

"Someone's supper sure smells good," he thought.

The curved roofs of the wigwams and longhouses showed black in the starlight. The embers of dying summer cook fires winked at them through the darkness. But the village was not yet sleeping. Dozens of human conversations, droned indistinguishably over the water, like the drowsy persistent hum of a distant beehive.

Suddenly something splashed the water to the right of the canoe, hitting Solomon with the spray. The boys paused for a second, until a muffled chuckle broke the stillness from the shadows along the shore. Jorris turned his paddle in his hand directing his craft a bit left, and the boys continued the silent cadence of their light, easy strokes.

In the starlight ahead, Solomon could see the dark tree line of the Benakill widen, once again preparing to rejoin the west branch. Here the island forms a long point of sand and silt jutting out into the wider water and then gradually disappearing again, into the river.

On the sand bar he saw a crisp, brightly burning little fire. As they drew nearer people were outlined moving in front of the blaze. Suddenly, feminine laughter came skipping across the water to greet them.

❦

As they glided up near the shore Solomon shipped his paddle. On stiff legs he rose, stepping to the sand as gracefully as any shore bird. Jorris followed, beaching the canoe so it would not drift.

As Jorris began to straighten up he saw a flash of dark skin and something solid and meaty hit him hard in the shoulder, pushing him toward the water. He was not quite standing and his center of gravity was yet low. With his feet planted wide, he spun his body away and ducked. Then, as the attacker passed over him, he came up hard pushing the unwelcome weight with its own momentum toward the river.

With a splash, the crowd from the fire erupted into squeals of laughter. An Indian boy laid now on his back, with his left leg half in the water. He seemed stunned. But then his mouth spread wide in a good-natured grin. He reached his hand toward Jorris. Jorris grabbed on to his wrist pulling him to his feet.

"How are you friend?" said the Indian.

"I'm fine Otter, but you're wet," Jorris replied.

"Otters like the water," said one of the girls, as most of the group turned and casually sauntered the few paces back to their fire.

The crowd gathered here, tonight, was larger than usual. There were ten boys and four young women, most in their early teens. Solomon, being only eleven, knew he was the youngest of the group by two years. Twisted-stalk and Red-corn were here and they were twelve. But they would not have been asked along if not for their connection to Jorris's little brother.

These were mostly Jorris's friends. There were other such hunting groups in the tribe. Some of these young men shifted back and forth among those different hunting parties. But Tobacco-spit, Otter, Big-nose and Jorris always seemed to be found together. It seemed to Solomon, that lately, Willow, June-bug, Blossom and Basket were also frequently being invited along when girls could be of help.

Tonight the group planned to fish for eel. The young women would be the torchbearers. Light from those torches would draw eel to the slaughter, like a moth to a flame.

Tobacco-spit and Big-nose paced the shoreline watching both branches of the river, while the others waited around the fire. The small fire was kindled only for its light, and carefully tended by the young women. They kept it built tall and the flames leapt high. Such a fire created the maximum amount of dancing light, with a minimum amount of wood, smoke, and heat.

Summer fires like this, were often built by young women of their tribe. They knew these fires could have magic effects. Sometimes if the moon was right, young men would notice beauty for the first time. They would see it, when the firelight danced in the darkness of a young maiden's eyes. Tonight was no different. More than one young man around that fire, felt its effects.

Abruptly from upriver, came the call of a goose. That was strange. Geese were usually expected to be far north this time of summer. Everyone smiled. The late members of their fishing party were arriving. One of the boys answered quickly: "Caw! Caw! Caw!" sounding exactly like a daytime crow, which by this time of night should have been expected to be quietly asleep in their tree top roosts.

Instantly laughter bubbled through the group as they burst into final preparations for the night's adventure. In moments the fire was doused, the gear loaded and they were boarding three bark canoes and the one large dugout, which had just arrived.

Solomon retrieved his paddle from the little bark and resumed his position in its bow. But just before Jorris pushed their craft off into the water, someone else slipped into their canoe. She assumed the same posture as Solomon, but just behind the center thwart.

It was dark, but he knew by the light step and graceful manner it was Willow sitting behind him. He was glad. He liked the girl.

More importantly he knew Jorris liked her. Nothing was said. Nothing needed to be said. With a firm push Jorris launched the canoe and they glided smoothly out into the dark, wet, river.

※

The fishing party beached their canoes at a shoal a few miles downstream. The place was almost half way to the Shawnee town at Pa-ha-quary. Two of the girls, each with a torch, positioned themselves out in the middle of the river, about 15 yards apart. The boys stationed themselves inside each circle of light, but facing the darkness.

Each of the young men held a gig or a special club used for this fishing. They waited. They watched the water.

The eels were partially blinded by the light, but they were curious. They approached slowly. But they did come. The action was sporadic, but, when it happened, it was wild and noisy and fun.

The Pine torches burned brightly that evening. Each torch had been carefully crafted, with five pieces of split yellow pine surrounding and extending above a center pole. The pine pieces oozed a sticky resin, which provided the fuel. Held carefully such torches could burn almost an hour, had anyone had a clock, with which to time them. All these youngsters knew was that they lasted long enough.

In the blackness that was the river valley this night, the torches cast an eerily dancing light, reflecting as they did off the moving water. Eel were not the only creatures to investigate.

A panther watched for a time from the safety of a near-by tree. But the fishermen cast shadows, with strange, quick, movements, making her flinch and growl softly. Soon she left the river, slinking through the trees toward the meadow.

A coyote pack came to drink and paused to watch. But the human howls held no meaning for them. They too trotted off.

In time all the creatures of this night and place witnessed the odd human behaviors. But, seeing no advantage to themselves they soon went about their own nighttime hunting.

Big-nose lit the last two torches in the very early hours of the next morning. He handed them to Laurel-flower and Basket. Solomon looked at the faces in the light. Red-corn and Twisted-stalk were still among the smiling faces awaiting the next round of action. But Solomon realized not everyone was still fishing. Among the missing, were Jorris and Willow.

Solomon turned away from the light, looking out into the darkness. His eyes adjusted and he could see that someone had kindled another small fire on shore. People were visible now moving in front of that blaze. Only about half the original fishing-party were still in the river. Solomon knew that some fisherman always lost interest as the night grew long. But Jorris had never been one to give up early.

Finally the last torch burned itself out. The weary fishermen drug themselves out of the river and called it a night. Dog-tired and wet Solomon waded to shore finding his blanket in the canoe. Jorris's blanket was gone.

Again, Solomon peered into the dark night, engulfing him. The small fire which had been burning on shore was only a few glowing embers now. No one was going to bother feeding it on such a warm night.

By the light of the stars he found a place well up on the sand and lay down curling up into the warmth of his wool blanket. The blanket itched a little, but its warmth was welcome to the wet youngster even on such a warm summers evening.

Closing his eyes he listened to the sounds of the big moving river—gentle waves—quiet, rhythmic—slapping against the sandy shore. In the distance he heard a whip-poor-will continue its repeating call: "whip-poor-will, whip-poor-will, whip-poor-will."

Solomon yawned. The damp night air spoke to him. It told of decaying fish, fresh flowing waters, wildflowers, grasses, muddy riverbanks, tall trees, deep forests and hot summer days.

He slept—the deep sleep of a tired, young boy, content in the only world he knew.

Chapter 9: To the Susquehanna

Two hours before sunset on 1 July 1719, a party of nine mounted men crossed the river at Kendiamong, riding quickly up to the Davids' cabin. It was Jake, Three-tongues, Wetherill, a new man named Harrison, and four others of the original party: Joseph Kirkbride, John Reading, James Steel and Jacob Taylor. Riding with them was a black slave named Toby who belonged to Harrison.

From where they worked in the hay field Pa and Solomon saw the riders. They watched them coming on but neither father nor son paused their mowing. This hay had to get cut before dark. Two of the men dismounted at the cabin, advancing on foot across the field toward them.

"Let us spell you a bit, Sol," said John Reading, reaching for the scythe held in Solomon Sr.'s sweat-stained hands.

Tom Wetherill reached for the boys scythe. Soon both men had taken up the tools swung all afternoon by the sunbaked father and son. The new hands bent quickly to the task, knowing well how that work was done.

The men left at the cabin unsaddled the horses. Soon they too tramped out, through the stubble of newly mowed grass, to give a hand. There were only two scythes, but the work progressed now much quicker. With so many hands, the tools never rested.

Jake brought along another jug from the springhouse. The men talked, laughed, drank, and worked. The two scythes whispered softly and steadily until it was so dark in the valley that even the meadowlarks had stopped singing. Lightening bugs rose now, like tiny blinking stars, floating casually upward. A smell of newly mowed grass greeted the cooler night air.

The men quit working. They trudged back toward the barn, their chatter and drinking never missing a beat. Washing up, at the water-trough, behind the springhouse, brought new laughter. Then, one by one, they sauntered off toward the smells of baking cornbread and frying fish.

The talk that evening was about the expedition. "Things aren't going so well." Joseph Kirkbride explained. "There are disagreements among the commissioners about our purpose. There's discord between them and the surveyors. Hell, the surveyors don't see eye-to-eye, even on the charts to be used to do the calculations.

This very morning the New York surveyors started a fight with their own commissioners. After some reeeal hot back-and-forth's everyone was pretty riled up. I can tell you. I swear, for a while, I thought it was going to turn to fisticuffs."

The men listening, who had been present, laughed, and John Reading saw Kirkbride pause. He seized that as his opportunity to jump into the conversation.

"You should have been there Sol," he said, his voice cracking with the humor of it.

"I swear, I thought Dr. Johnston and Mr. Willocks were both going to have a spell or something. Their faces were both as red as an old tom turkey's beard."

Reading chuckled a bit and then his countenance changed.

"You know we can deal with the skeeters, the rough country and the short rations. But we didn't come all this way, over these mountains, to waste our damn time arguing over stuff that should have been sorted out long ago, by them that sent us."

He was serious now. His tone had changed. The smile was gone.

"We're here to get this job done. Now, it's our reputations on the line. And I don't like this committee decision-making we're being forced to endure. By-Damn this is important…"

Solomon Jr. began to tune out the conversation, drifting off into his own thoughts. He had never seen a black man before. He had heard about them. But none had ever come to his valley. Until today.

He had stared, when first he saw the black man walking across the hay field. But when the black man had met his gaze, the boy had averted his eyes. From that time, Solomon had watched the black slyly, steeling glimpses, when he could.

He learned quickly that Toby went wherever Harrison went. Toby didn't talk much. Harrison did his talking for him. The black man, was however, a willing worker, keeping himself busy in the field and around the cabin?

Toby smiled often that evening, each time he looked up to see the boy watching him. But, Toby finally tired of the conversation too. He rolled his eyes and yawned. As Reading drew a breath to continue his diatribe, Toby said:

"Excuse me sirs."

He rose quietly and strode out the door on his way to the barn. No one noticed him go, but the boy.

The next morning broke with overcast skies. A gentle west-breeze greeted each person, as he awoke to the unmistakable, refreshing smell of rain. Beyond the Pennsylvania mountains the distant rumble of some far off storm was clear.

Kirkbride, Reading, Steel, Taylor and Wetherill saddled up early. Jake, Three-tongues, Harrison and Toby came out of the barn ready for the woods. Each man carried a heavy possible bag and a light wool blanket, rolled up in oiled canvas, slung across his shoulders. Jake, Three-tongues and Harrison carried muskets, but Toby had only a pistol and a tomahawk in his belt.

The whole party walked to the river, leaving behind the saddled, but still hobbled horses. Solomon Sr. and Wetherill carried Jorris's small bark canoe. When they reached the river Solomon Jr. ferried across, in turn, each of the four men, with their gear.

The wind began to kick up. Choppy little ripples covered the water, though not yet what anyone might call waves, let alone white caps. The storm was still a-ways off, but nobody had any doubt it was coming.

As Solomon reached the New Jersey shore, on his final return, Pa and Wetherill hoisted the canoe. Everyone trudged back toward the cabin.

The boy hesitated. The thunder grumbled. He glanced westward across the Fishkill just as Jake waved. Then Solomon noted how small the men looked, standing in the distance, beside the gigantic trees, with those dark clouds rolling over the mountains.

It was a poor morning to be starting out on a long hunt. Solomon Jr. swung his whole arm returning their salute. Then all four men on the west bank, disappeared, one by one, into the primeval forests of eighteenth century Pennsylvania. It would be a long trek, and where they were heading, horses would do them no good.

Back at the cabin the other visitors bridled and mounted their horses, heading off for Decker's at a slow trot. Reading paused, as he sat his horse, and looked down at Solomon Sr..

"Good luck with your hay Sol. Looks like it's going to have a tough time drying."

Solomon Sr. nodded with a hang-dog look and glanced off toward the rolling dark clouds.

"Looks like we're gonna need luck of our own," Reading continued. "Decker is guiding us to Coshecton when we get back. Hopefully, we'll find our station somewhere near there. I'm told it's a rough piney country. And we're going to move the whole shebang, if we can keep them from killing each other before they get there".

He laughed kicking his horse, lightly, in the belly, and galloping off to catch up with the other riders. As he rode away, when no one else could see, Reading's smile gradually changed to a look of steady determination.

Chapter 10: Coshecton

A few days later, the hay was stacked, on the Davids' plantation, before the big rain began. But when the rain came in July 1719, it came to stay. When it wasn't raining, it was threatening rain. Day and night it was drizzly, storming, or heavy with fog. Except for brief periods, the sky was cloudy for two solid weeks. In moments between the rain, farmers of the valley struggled to get their wheat cut, dried and in the shocks.

Slogging in muddy fields the men toiled. It was bad weather for farmers. But conditions were even worse for surveyors.

After a hard day's traverse toward Coshecton, it was clear to all in the expedition that it would be a tough trip. Most of the men were in their bedrolls, when John Reading reached for his journal and writing tools. Kirkbride snorted and snored intermittently, from his bedroll a few feet on the other side of their campfire, which was still burning brightly.

"I'll just write a few words," Reading whispered aloud, to himself, as he sat down on the ground near the fire.

From a small, well crafted, walnut, box he procured his leather backed journal, a quill pen, an ink blotter, and a tiny light-brown, earthenware ink-well. He positioned these items on a clean mossy site just beside himself, so he could see them all clearly by the light of the fire. Deliberately he secured the mottled, stoneware vessel against accidental spills, by placing three flat rocks snug against and surrounding it. Good ink was hard to come by on the trail. He was not a man to take unnecessary risk.

He made himself as comfortable as possible leaning his back against his bedroll which was propped now against a hog-sized bolder conveniently place here for him by ancient glaciers. He situated the storage box as a wooden lap desk and placed his journal upon it. Opening the journal he thumbed the pages until he found where he had left off writing last night, and stared at the blank page before him, his eyes adjusting to the light. His mind settled to the task. He dipped his quill-pen into the ink, and began his script.

"July 8th: This Morning Dr. Johnston coming, departed all our company from Mahackmech, stored with provisions for the surveyors recruit, being accompanied with J. Decker and two other Dutchmen....." (Reading, 1915)

He looked up, listening to the crackle of the fire. A frog croaked somewhere outside the light of their camp. Reading stretched his arms above his head with a yawn and then returned to his writing for a few minutes more. He paused then, for another moment, staring thoughtfully off into the darkness. Dipping his pen into the ink, he finished his journal entry for that day by penning:

"The land (If it be proper to call it so) in this day's journey is most excessive stony, little else but pine timber, some of which are very good for spars, being white pine, exceeding tall but not very big. We crossed several excessive precipices, none that we crossed but which were very stony and commonly attended with pine swamps under grown with lawrel and bay bushes." (Reading, 1915)

Carefully he blotted his last writing. He waited another moment, to be certain the ink had dried, closed his journal, set it aside, corked his ink well, stored all his materials back in the walnut box, pulled his blanket over his shoulders and quickly faded off to sleep.

The next day's journey was much the same as the day before only more extreme. That night the expedition made camp before dusk. Reading soon sat with his back against a small clump of iron wood trees, writing once more in his journal, this time by the dimming light of a grey cloudy day.

It was hot and steamy this evening. The gnats and mosquitoes were abundant and woefully aggressive.

"It's maddening", he thought, "to have these little buggers buzzing your ear as you try to write."

But John Reading being a man of purpose did not write of insects. This evening he put his pen to the paper and wrote:

"July 9th having had an indifferent nights rest in the morning we prosecuted our intended journey through very stony high mountains and steep precipices, not having met in our journey heretofore with such bad way and much of it..." (Reading, 1915)

Then after several paragraphs, describing the day's events, he paused putting down the pen and finally swatted a particularly annoying mosquito. He picked up the pen and wrote:

"Through such difficulties which none knows and few can imagine but those that have had the trial. At last we arrived at the Indian plantations called Coshecton, being seated in a pleasant valley on both sides of the river." (Reading, 1915)

―※―

The expedition had passed through the Munsi village with only slight delay for introduction and presentations of gifts to the village elders. Hoping for some privacy the white men forded the river and continued upstream another two miles before establishing their temporary camp in an open stand of river birch and cottonwoods. They had arrived at Coshecton, thirty miles west-northwest of Decker's farm, accompanied by a thunder-gust. To their consternation the clouds, the local Munsi and the mosquitoes followed them upstream to their new camp and never left.

Every time a canoe load of local Indians departed another canoe load or two or maybe three arrived. Despite the language barrier there was the continuous babble of trade, eagerly sought by the local natives. At night most of the Munsi returned to their homes, but always a few slept nearby beneath their canoes. It all seemed harmless enough but it put a strain on provisions.

Now it was a week later. The expedition was running low on supply. A few moments ago the sky had cleared and despite the late hour of the day everyone was rushing to get the equipment set up for an observation.

Suddenly one of the local elders, a man named Blue-hat, leaped forward snatching the English quadrant[5] from the hand of John Reading. He stepped quickly away with a menacing gesture.

Everyone was stunned for a second or two. Then, eyes narrowed. The seriousness of the situation settled upon them. Over the next few seconds, each man formulated his plan for survival. But, no one moved.

Instinct took over. The situation was not quite yet out of control. Much would depend on what happened next.

Eyes flashed from face to face and around the camp. There was no line of battle. Neither group had planned for a fight.

Weapons were scattered about. Some hung in belts and sheaths, others were on the ground, or in the tents. Men, who moments before had been smiling or talking one with another, suddenly realized, they might be killing each other in a few seconds more. Dr. Willox emitted a nervous laugh and little beads of sweat began popping out on his forehead and rolling down his plump red face.

John Chapman glanced quickly about, taking in as much information as he could. What just happened? Why? What the devil is wrong? Who has been offended? Which fool caused this?

No one moved.

---

[5] The most advanced navigational instrument of the time. Invented by Englishman John Davis in 1594.

Tom Wetherill smiled at Blue-hat from a few yards away. Then, still not moving, he asked: "Blue Hat, my old friend. Are you going to start the trading by grabbing our best piece?"

Blue-hat didn't smile. But, he spoke in a firm, clear voice. "No iron rope. No survey. No sell land."

"No... NO," said Wetherill. "We're not here to survey or buy your land. We just need to do some observations of the sky from here, because it is the best place to see from".

"No!" said Blue-hat. "White man trick Indian and steal land. Munsi knows where he live," he asserted.

With that said, Blue-hat turned, cautiously walking away with the instrument. As he did so, everyone seemed to breathe again. Eyes widened. Weight shifted. Slowly, very slowly, men began to move again.

Trying to appear casual, men who had been eyeing one another menacingly drew apart, sauntering away, each toward their own side, without ever really losing sight of the other.

Indians, and whites, soon segregated themselves into separate groups, murmuring quietly to each other. What had just happened? Why? Who caused it? What happens next?

It took a while to sort out, but gradually the Indians settled around cook-fires at the edge of the camp, and the whites huddled around the ones nearer the center. There were now a few guarded comments between groups, but the laughter was gone. Each man now knew where his weapons were. None were far from hand.

Suddenly Wetherill grunted, shook his head, and stomped off deliberately to the supply tent. Throwing back the flap, he ducked his head and entered. It was musty inside, dark and smelled of wet canvas. He could be heard rummaged about inside for a moment or two and then things got quiet.

The canvas door flap suddenly slapped back. Tom emerged carrying a small keg on his shoulder. The keg was marked clearly "Punch.[6] He strode quickly straight to where Blue-hat stood, under a little river birch, examining the English quadrant.

Blue-hat haphazardly fingered the adjustments on the strange instrument, with a very puzzled look on his face. That confused look only intensified as the old man watched, wide-eyed, as Wetherill approached him with the keg.

Tom stopped a few paces away from the elder and peered intently at the old chief. The Indian stopped fidgeting with the instrument and studied Wetherill's eyes. Then he glanced at the keg on Wetherill's shoulder—back to Wetherill's eyes—back to the keg.

"I thought Blue-hat would want to take this gift, to share with his bothers down river in the lodges of his people," said Wetherill. Without waiting for an answer he said, "I'll just put it in your canoe so you will not forget to take it when you're ready to go."

He passed by the old man and strolled straight toward the river where several bark and dugout canoes were hauled up on a little sand bar. He did not look back as he walked. But he could hear footsteps following him. From the rustling of the leaves on the forest floor he could tell there was more than one man hastening along.

After depositing the keg into the canoe he turned to face Blue-hat. Forty pair of thirsting, incredulous, dark eyes stared back at him. No one smiled.

The silence was pervasive. It screamed out: "Be cautious. Careful now. You're almost home."

Wetherill stared back at Blue-hat with the honest, bold visage of a man who had known danger before and met it again now, fairly, and with complete understanding. He waited. A

---

[6] Punch = common term for a blend of whiskey and other alcoholic-spirits of the time.

red-winged blackbird sang from the reeds somewhere across the river.

"Yes," said Blue-hat "Must go now. Come back tomorrow."

With that he reached down dropping the quadrant with a thump into the bottom of the craft. He pushed the canoe out into the river. Gracefully he stepped into the dugout and sat down, as two younger men boarded, assuming the paddling positions, aft and stern. In moments the whole party of Indians were in their canoes, paddling rapidly downstream toward a big bend in the river on their way home for a celebration.

Wetherill watched until the last canoe disappeared from sight. His legs felt suddenly weak. His broad shoulders shuddered like a horse sheading flies. Then, he exhaled slowly and took a deep breath.

When Wetherill turned to trudge up the riverbank, he was greeted by several of his smiling companions, who had come to witness the departure.

There was more than one quadrant in the survey party, but the clouds had returned. There would be no observations accomplished now. So the men busied themselves cooking supper and tending to other chores.

Nothing much was said but every man in camp knew something had changed. The night-watch picked from that day forward, were always, men experienced in the wilderness. But on this night the whole company slept a little easier, knowing the Munsi were whooping it up, far downriver, hopefully not thinking about surveys.

Next morning the drizzle and fog set in for another day. The expedition did not have a plan for such conditions. The Commissioners continued to argue and offend one another. The country was rocky. Horses threw their iron shoes or their shoes became so loose that they had to be removed. Harnesses broke. Food spoiled.

The men got little sleep on nights, when the thunder-gusts really turned loose. The 'whole shebang' had been here a sodden week, but not a single celestial observation had been confirmed. Tempers were getting as short as the food supplies. There was little that could be done but wait for another clear sky.

Blue-hat and his braves returned, sharing venison and eel with the white men, but the supplies continued to dwindle.

Reading and Wetherill decided to visit the Munsi village on one particularly rainy day. As they trudged into the village from the river Wetherill noticed two Munsi men at a distance stitching up something, which at first appeared to be a very heavy canvas. He poked Reading, nodding toward the men. They sauntered toward the work being done.

As they approached they noticed the ribs and gunnels, which had previously been heated and bent into shape. These oak pieces had been ingeniously formed into the frame for the canoe the Munsi were building. It was to be a river canoe so there was no keel. Instead there was a completely rounded bottom.

The builders were working swiftly with bone needles and sinew stitching together large sheets of elm-bark which lay in a stack on the ground near-by. The braves or someone-else in the village had earlier stripped this bark from the biggest trees they could find. As they worked the braves were attaching the bark to the frame as the outer skin for the craft.

It was precision work accomplished with the crudest tools. But judging by the canoes they had already witnessed on the river, Wetherill had no doubt it would give long and useful service, once all its seems had been amply sealed with pine-pitch.

It was an admirable and ancient design. It had evolved specifically for use in fast waters, like those of the upper Fishkill. Wetherill was impressed. He nodded approvingly at the two workmen who smiled back proudly. Wetherill and Reading walked on to visit the Village elders.

On 16 July John Reading approached Tom Wetherill at one of the breakfast fires. With each raindrop, the fire smoldered and hissed in front of a small, canvas lean-to. The smoke hung low this morning, barely rising from the ground. It mixed with the fog, staining faces and burning eyes. The men endured trying to stay a little bit dry. It was a muddy, wet, morning and it looked to be the same all day, as it had been the day before, and for all the days since they got here.

Reading wasted no time getting to the point.

"Tom—Kirkbride, Steel and I are leavin' today. Most of the men and horses will be comin' with us. The commissioners have all agreed. They want you, Decker, and a surveyor from each colony, to stay behind, with what remains of the food stuffs—to see if you can get the job done."

Reading hesitated and looked at his friend. Wetherill nodded, but said nothing. Instead, he continued picking at the dry corn meal and fried eel, he was choking down for breakfast.

"I know I don't have to tell you this, Tom, but this is still mighty important business. If you don't have so many mouths to feed, you may be able to stay long enough to get it done. I'd stay with you, but if I stay—the blasted Yorkers won't go. The whole deal falls apart. Nobody trusts anybody."

Reading looked off toward Dr. Johnston, a New York commissioner, who stood watching him from a nearby fire. Johnston was a portly man, with wild disheveled hair on this morning. Reading imagined him at home in Kingston proudly maintaining a plump clean-shaven face and well groomed gray hair, when not wearing his powdered wig. Johnston had not traveled well. His scraggly gray beard, sweating cheeks and un-kept scalp made him appear today, more a savage than the gentleman he purported to be.

Dr. Johnston was not happy to be here. He was determined they were too far north for this to be a good place to establish the boundary. Too many powerful men in Kingston stood to loose money.

He had been unable to control these men here from the Jersey's as he had promised his superiors he would do. This morning with a furrowed brow he stared at Reading talking to Wetherill. He was trusting that the sky would not clear in time so they all could just go home and try again in another expedition a few years hence, when he or others might better influence the outcome to New York's advantage.

Suspiciously he watched Reading talk to Wetherill, clinging to the prospect that the latter might refuse his assignment. After all, when the bulk of the expedition left Coshecton the remaining few men would be completely at the mercy of the local savages.

"You get on pretty well with Blue-hat," said Reading to Wetherill. "Decker has convinced him to bring you all down by canoe, when the job is done. We'll have to pay him and his boys in punch and trade goods. But everyone has agreed, it's our best chance. The Indians seem to have forgotten about surveys. Just don't let anyone act too much like a survey feller, or ask too many questions about the land, or smell any dirt."

Reading chuckled to himself when he thought about what he had said. Wetherill made no response. So Reading went on.

"Maybe they won't notice when the observations finally get made."

He smiled at his old friend and nodded toward a couple of braves trotting through the trees toward the river. Wetherill watched the braves disappear into the laurel bushes then turned back to his plate.

"Shoot, they're out roamin' the woods most of the time anyway," said Reading. "Decker swears they're friendly and they act calm enough. He says they can be counted on to get you down to his place whenever you're ready. I reckon he ought to know, he hunts and trades with 'em all the time."

"Okay", said Tom, peering up from under his hat brim, his keen, hazel eyes clearly accepted the challenge of this new plan.

"I'm getting tired of all the bickering and fussin' anyhow. With the 'Gentlemen' gone maybe we can get some business done, and sure as the devil, it will be more peaceable".

Wetherill looked down and went back again to picking at his food. Reading started to say something else. But, thought better of it, smiled to himself, and walked off toward the horses.

An hour later that morning, Joseph Kirkbride, James Steel, John Reading and most of the whole shebang mounted their horses. Without a word Reading turned his horse southeast and started him down the trail. The nearby woods came alive suddenly with the jingle of bridle bits, the squeak of saddle leather, and the steady stomp of heavy hooves. A few minutes later the last of those sounds faded off into the forest. It was quiet. A squirrel soon began cutting on an acorn from somewhere above and dropping pieces through the leaf canopy to the ground below.

The job was still not done. Reading and his party had taken all but two of the horses with them, intending that most of the remaining surveyors would return with John Decker and the Indians by canoe.

Everyone knew this was their final maneuver. If this didn't work, they would fail. It all depended upon when the sky might clear, the help of John Decker and the good will of the local savages.

Chapter 11: The Blacksmith

Eight miles was a long ride on a wet foggy morning.

Solomon Jr. rode double behind his father on the big grey gelding. A separate piece of oiled sailcloth shielded each of them from the drizzly rain.

The redolence of sweaty horsehair rose in a warm steam under the ponchos. The boy held on lightly and the warmth of the big animal, felt against his legs, was not unwelcome this wet morning. The big gelding slogged up the road at a graceful pace, steadily covering the distance. Over his father's shoulder, Solomon could see the destination, and the open doors of the blacksmiths' barn were a welcome sight.

"Morning Sol," he heard Mr. Cole say as they rode in. "Mornin' Solomon," he heard him add.

"Morning," they both responded at once.

"Daniel, we're wet and the horse needs shod," said Solomon Sr. as they dismounted. "We thought we would pick up a real set of hinges and one of those fancy little candle holders you've been makin' lately."

They led their horse inside the barn, tying the bridle reins to a post. The boy loosened the cinch and girth straps, the father removed the saddle and blanket. The grey shuddered, flicked its tail in response and let out a deep sigh.

Then, suddenly, the horse and the dismounted riders, broke the inside stillness, stamping their feet and shaking as much rain from their backs as they could shake. Eyes adjusted to the darker surroundings and Solomon Jr. edged himself toward the small, red glow of a coke-fire, he noticed burning in the forge. The blacksmith spoke up.

"Well Sol, I can fix you up with a candle holder fer' the wife. But I'm out of iron for anything else! At least till I can get to Sopus[7] and back, lessen' you brought some scrap with you?"

"Damn!" Solomon Sr. responded. "We didn't figure on that."

"Well, business has been uncommonly good of late, with all these goings on," the smith explained.

"I don't usually shoe morn' a horse a month. But these survey fellers have cleaned me out of Iron. They're rough on horses and they want em' well shod."

"The other day they darn near lost a whole horse, in a sink hole north of here. It took four men, some block and tackle, and three other horses, half a day just to get the poor beast out. She may never be sound again. They got her on pasture down there at Decker's." He added spitting into the straw.

"Have they set that station point yet?" Solomon Sr. asked.

"Well, some say yes, and some say no!" The blacksmith continued with a wink and wry little smile directed at the boy. "Swartwood was in here yesterday. He says they're all wrong lookin' way up near Coshecton."

The blacksmith dipped oats with a maple measure from a large walnut grain-bin into a small oak bucket, and hung the bucket from an iron hook, in the post, where the horse was tied.

"You know how it is Sol, everbody has an idea about it. The one they like best is the one they stand to gain from. One of them surveyor fellers says it's goin' to get set, whether the Yorkers like it or not. I just hope it gets done before somebody gets killed."

The horse snorted, sniffed the bucket, stuck his nose into it and began to munch on the grain.

---

[7] Sopus was a common term for Esopus. Both names were still used locally for decades after the town was officially renamed Kingston following the Dutch surrendered the territory to the English in 1664.

"Heck, Tuesday a week ago, some jackasses from Goshen come over the mountain and took all of Westfall's wheat. Hauled it off, toward Kingston, still in the shock. Westfall swears he'll get even! I recon he'll be askin' his neighbors fer' help," the blacksmith added, gazing out of his barn at the falling rain.

Solomon Sr. shook his head.

"Well, Johannes don't have to ask. He just has to say when. The boys from Goshen may find they have come over that pass, to collect taxes, once too often.

Solomon Jr. listened wondering what his father intended to do. The conversation changed then to talk of how the corn was growing, horses lost and found, the condition of the road, and who had packed up to move back to Marbletown or Kingston or somewhere else. An hour passed quickly. The grey gelding rested himself munching on the grain in the bucket and later on some hay, Solomon Jr. raked down for him, from the loft.

Too soon it seemed, they were re-mounted, heading out of the barn toward home, with only some news and a small candleholder for the trouble of a long wet ride. At least the rain had stopped. But the sky remained gray.

The pair were quiet as they rode south. Two miles along the road, they came to the Decker place. It was a small fieldstone house with a steep shake roof, set off to the left, on slightly elevated ground, a short distance from the Machackemack Branch and a mile north of where the road forded that little stream. There was also a large stone barn, smoke-house, and springhouse. John Decker was a good farmer with a large family.

Solomon Jr. did not notice the house at first. The gentle swaying gate of the horse and the steady echoing pattern of heavy clomping hooves, beneath him, had lulled him into a daze. He awoke suddenly, when he noticed Mrs. Decker gazing out at the approaching riders from a Dutch door, the bottom half of which remained closed.

This morning the Decker farm had seemed abnormally quiet as they had ridden past. One of the Decker boys had run out then, to say his Pa was back from Coshecton, but sick. This time Solomon Sr. reined the grey into the lane and trotted the horse quickly up to the doorway.

"Morning Solomon," said Mrs. Decker as they rode up.

"Morning," they answered in unison.

Mrs. Decker opened the bottom door stepping out, with the whisper of a barefoot little girl not more than three-year-old following. The mother of the Decker clan was a slight woman approaching forty. Today she displayed dark circles, under her tired blue eyes and a furrowed brow. The child kept a firm grip on her mothers' skirt, behind which she tried to keep herself hidden.

"Morning Miss Lea," said Solomon Sr. to the little blond girl who peeked out briefly from behind the skirt, flashing big, sparkling, blue eyes, set in a fair round face, with a sweet smile. Then she disappeared almost immediately behind her mother again.

"John is sleepin'," said Mrs. Decker. "He has the fever. I wish he had stayed to home. And let someone else do the guidin' work. Our hay hasn't been cut. And half the wheat is rotting in the field."

She brushed her hair back with a sigh, glancing beyond the barn toward the partially cut wheat field.

"What the boys did manage to cut is molding, 'stead of drying," she said.

The clouds were riding so low now, that here and there, they came down to touch the ground and roll mysterious and ominously across the fields and pastures of John Decker's little farm. "Will this rain ever stop?" Asked Mrs. Decker, looking up at the darkening sky.

But before they could answer she went on. Nodding to the northward she said,

"You boys better get on across the river. It rises fast when it rains heavy in those hills."

She swirled about, without waiting for an answer. She led the little girl inside, calling back over her shoulder as she did,

"We'll get together when the sun shines."

She closed the doors behind her with two hollow thumps.

Solomon Sr. turned the grey and urged him into a brisk trot toward the ford. Solomon Jr. waved back at three of the Decker boys, who he saw then running across their wheat field, toward the barn.

A few minutes later, Solomon and his father reached the ford. The river was rising as Mrs. Decker had said it would. The gray day flickered with bright flashes of light and across the distance the thunder rumbled, slowly reverberating then toward them, from over the hills to the North.

They crossed the little river quickly, avoiding a swim, which would have been required a few minutes later. A drizzly rain began once more to fall upon them. The sky grew darker. The two Solomon Davids, pulled their hats lower and rode their big grey horse toward home at the lowland meadow called Kendiamong.

Late that afternoon the Machackemack River ran bank full in most places and here and there overflowed its' banks. John Decker's canoe, left unattended near the river, drifted away as he lay sick in his bed. As sometimes happens, the rising waters of the river on this night, proved a force, which could not be denied. It swept everything before it, on into the warm, foggy, July darkness.

Chapter 12: The Run-away

The sun was already high, maybe ten of the clock. The panther had returned to her rocky lair in the high country. The Red-tail circled over-head. It was a hot sticky day, as the boy strolled up the muddy, spongy trail, from the river toward the cabin. His moccasins squished with every careful step.

The grass glistened with droplets from last nights rain. A warm, muggy steam rose from the meadow. Behind him, somewhere not far off, Solomon heard the distinctive chatter of a kingfisher in one of its familiar, undulating, flights along the river. It was a pleasant morning.

Moments before, in his canoe, Solomon Jr. had ferried Three-tongues and Jake to the western shore. They were heading up the Pennsylvania trail toward Coshecton looking for the remaining surveyors. This day was what his Pa called a blue-bird day, one without a cloud in the sky, except for maybe a wisp here and there, which just couldn't seem to hold together.

Jake, Three-tongues and the man named Harrison had been back from the Susquehanna almost a week. Everyone also knew that most of the expedition had returned from Coshecton. They were back to their lodgings at Decker's, Westphalia's and Swartwood's. Only a few men remained out trying to conclude their business.

In the past few days Jake had told and retold the story of guiding Harrison and his man Toby to the Susquehanna. They had gone all the way to the Wyoming Valley. To make the most of the trip, Jake said, they had made a few trades with the local Shawnee before starting back.

Harrison was well satisfied with the information they had gathered; which was exactly as Solomon Sr. had told them all, before they left, that it would be. There was no larger branch of the Delaware River west of the Fishkill. Harrison would now officially attest to that fact.

As Solomon Jr. rambled along he wondered about the man named Toby. Toby had not returned with the others. Toby had run away.

Solomon had known run-aways before, but they had always been white men, running from indentures and harsh treatment. Toby had seemed happy enough, when he was here a short time ago, smiling and working with the others in the hay field. He had been quiet. But he had seemed content with his station.

Then, Solomon had not really thought about Toby's life as a slave. Now, he thought about it some. He guessed it might not have been all that good, no matter how much the man smiled.

A small dark shadow floated suddenly across the grassland passing directly over the boy. Solomon looked up to see the red-tailed-hawk soaring above him in the brilliant clarity of a bright blue sky.

"So you want to play?" said Solomon.

The bird never heard his words, but she continued to glide across the sky in a wide circle. She was riding thermal winds, up and then down, catching first one and then another. On days like this, the spiraling air currents of this valley could keep a hawk gliding for most of the day so long as she kept a sharp watch-out for eagles.

Solomon had decided long ago that the shadow fly-overs were not accidental. They happened too often to be coincidence. He had concluded it was a simple game the hawk liked to play with creatures who could not fly and who were too big for a hawk to eat.

Hours passed. The day remained clear. Three riders suddenly appeared on the road heading south toward the cabin. They cast long shadows to the eastward as they moved steadily toward Kendiamong.

Men came then from within the cabin. Human voices rang out across the distance in greeting. A light wind rustled the grass. The sun sank toward the western ridgeline across the river.

Soon the last arc of the red globe disappeared, a rosy afterglow taking its place. The Thermals died away and the red-tailed hawk vanished.

But it was not yet dark. Nighthawks now came skittering through the sky, their distant cries barely audible. Three of the men emerged again from the cabin. One mounted his horse riding north and the human voices rang out once more over the meadow.

The panther watched all this at a distance. The two men left standing in front of the cabin led their horses to the barn. From within, muffled noises reverberated for a short time and then things quieted and those men strolled back to the cabin.

As they pulled open the door, a dim mellow light shone, but it was not yet dark enough outside, for the cat to see clearly within. Laughter and human smells drifted once more into the open air. But when the door closed, the crickets and peepers began their nightly chorus and the panther padded away, into the night.

Chapter 13: The Hatchet

Next morning, John Harrison and John Reading stood outside the cabin, with Solomon Davids. Solomon Jr. was there too, holding the reins of their saddled horses. The animals sniffed the bare ground, occasionally shifted their weight, or flicked at a fly with their tail, as they patiently awaited the day's work.

"I dang near forgot," said Reading, stepping to the side of his horse and fumbling with the straps on his saddlebag. He reached inside, feeling for something. He pulled out his hand and brought forth a rusty hatchet head. He presented it to Solomon Sr. with a self-satisfied smile and a question on his face.

"What do you think?" asked Reading.

Solomon took the object and looked it over carefully. It had some heft to it and was shrouded in a thick, rough, rusty, brown, oxidation.

"Well it's old, that's for sure."

"I found that at our campsite a couple nights back, comin' down from Coshecton," said Reading. "It was buried near the fire pit, with the blade edge up, but just barely above the surface. We walked over it all night; didn't see it till the next mornin'. It looked like it had been there a long time. Laurel roots had grown through the eye for some years I recon. Made it pretty hard to dig out, I can tell you. The boys all looked it over and it sure looked Dutch made to us. Do you think maybe your Grand-Pap, Old Christoffel Davids, his-self, might have lost it?"

"Maybe," said Solomon. "More likely he traded it to some brave who lost it, or died with it in his belt. See any bones nearby?"

"Didn't see any. Can't say for sure. We didn't do no digin' er nothin', except to get the hatchet head out." Said Reading.

Solomon Sr. turned the blade over in his hands examining it more closely. A puzzled look came to his face as he pondered the item.

"Maybe Old Christoffel did own it at one time," said Solomon. "He traded with the Munsi a lot in the 60's and 70's. Course he weren't the only Dutch trader—just one of em'. But he was one of the first, to trade with the people of this valley. And this hatchet does, sure as the devil, look Dutch made." He turned the rusty lump of iron over in his hands as if studying it for sign.

"Then again it could have been one of Pa's in the early years. Sure as heck too old to be one I traded. Too good an item, too. Smiths don't take as much time today."

"Is it for me to keep?" he asked.

"I brought it to you 'cause I knew you would appreciate it," said Reading.

"It's funny how often we travel the same paths as the old timers, ain't it. Sometimes we use the same camp sites and sleep under the same old trees, though they might not have been so tall when our forefathers slept under em'."

Reading turned and began retying his saddlebags. Solomon Sr. turned to John Harrison.

"Well, Harrison, I'll post your notice for you. But I doubt it will do any good. Most men who disappear into those woods on purpose, don't usually come back, for whatever reason. Some die. Some don't. But they don't usually come out—leastwise not at the same spot where they go in."

"Thank you Sol," said Harrison. "I know it's a long shot but if I can't get the ungrateful fellow back, I'd like to at least have the compass and gun. Anyway thanks for all your help."

Harrison reached out, taking the reins of his horse from the boy and mounting. John Reading stepped forward and shook hands with Solomon Sr.

"Good seeing you again Sol," he said. "When you come over to the Raritan, we'll tip another jug or two."

He took his reins from the boy. But then he offered his hand to Solomon Jr., looking down at the boy with a fondness in his eye. Solomon took his hand, and when they shook, the boy noticed Reading had the firm grip of a man who had known not only the surveyor's tools, but also the axe and the plow. Reading mounted, turning his horse north, but pulled up momentarily.

"Sol, Maybe you can bring that boy along next time you come, he can kill us some snakes to eat."

The men laughed as they rode away on the road toward the Machackemack Branch. It was the 24th of July 1719 and only the second day in almost a month, when it did not look like rain.

John Reading and John Harrison rode back that day to Decker's. For a few more days the whole expedition was back together and they were still arguing. Tom Weatherill and the last surveyors had returned from Coshecton. They claimed they had fixed the station on the river just to the south of where they all had camped but there was still plenty of debate about it.

After supper on July 25th Reading sat at a table, in John Decker's stone house, scribbling in his journal by the flickering light of two short candles.

"This is some better light than my usual accommodations." He thought, watching a giant brown moth fluttering near one of the candles. As he knew it would, soon it flew too close. It touched the flame, shriveled up, died, and was consumed.

Reading picked up his quill and wrote:

"25th July: This day the returns were drawn fair over and draughts of the station affixed thereto in order to be signed but several debates arising, and Capt. Waters indisposition and unwillingness to stay to complete the same, it was deferred till Monday morning. These debates were occasioned by the Yorkers refusing to sign until the work was completed, which seemed very unreasonable that we

should wait upon them to New York when we were not commissioned to do so..." (Reading, 1915)

※

Another day passed and on the evening of July 26ᵗʰ Reading sat at the same table in the same house. On the floor across the room Joseph Kirkbride lay on a pallet Mrs. Decker had arranged for him. He was sleeping finally. It had been some time since Reading had heard him jabbering incoherently or noticed him shivering so hard it shook the candles on the table. Carefully, Reading adjusted the position of the candles to best advantage for casting light onto his blank page. He dipped his quill into the ink well, twitched it back and forth in his fingers a couple times, gathering his thoughts, and began his entry for the day:

"*This day was spent at our landlord's, Joseph Kirkbride being very sick of the fever and ague, the Yorkers the day before removed to Thomas Swartwoots.*"(Reading, 1915)

※

Morning woke with a blue sky and the sharp cry of a catbird in the orchard. Kirkbride slept quietly. Reading's blankets sat rolled and tied in the corner of the room. Reading had left the house early.

Mrs. Decker stepped out her Dutch-door to find Wetherill at the hitching post, tossing his saddle onto the back of his big bay gelding.

"Mornin' ma'am," said Wetherill, touching the front of his hat brim. He reached under the belly of the horse and brought forth the cinch strap, inserting it into the metal ring on this side of his saddle. Not so gently, he nudged the gelding in the belly with his knee. When the horse expelled the breath it had been holding Wetherill cinched the strap tight.

"Will the Yorkers agree to your findings?" she asked.

"Reading thinks they will," he answered.

"What do you think?" she responded.

I don't know ma'am. Most of 'em will I think—but I don't trust Dr. Johnston. He's been trouble from the start. Soon as Reading finds his strayed horse I reckon we'll go find out."

Wetherill finished his knot with a sharp tug on the strap. Then he turned to face his questioner.

"I hope it gets settled now for your sakes. People here-abouts need a decision one way or another. Otherwise your peaceful little valley won't be so peaceful when families really start to grow; or when lots of new folks start showing up, all wanting a little farmstead of their own. Men always need clarity, when it comes to ownership of the land."

He turned back to reach under the horse again, this time for the girth strap, and began to buckle it to this side of the saddle.

"Sooner or later," he said, "the lawyers always show up, after a place gets settled…it may take another decade, or maybe two, but eventually they will get out to this valley. When they get here the only thing that will matter is clear ownership of the land. And that will depend on a good patent, sold to you by the people who had the King's right of possession. And who has that right will depend upon the location point we're trying to settle right now."

He fastened the girth strap buckle and turned to face her again.

"Heck you already got trouble, with New York and the Jerseys both trying to collect taxes from you, and both expecting your men folk to serve in their militias. Yeah, I hope it gets settled now for your sakes. You folks have been here a long time. You've worked hard to start these farms. You've earned the right to know where to pay your taxes and which militia to serve. You shouldn't have to argue with sheriffs trying to collect when you have already paid and done your duty."

Mrs. Decker sighed and looked off across the broad fields toward the river. Wetherill smiled.

"Hopefully we'll get all that settled once and forever, today," he said.

"Well, good luck then," she said, turning back inside.

"Good day, ma'am, and good luck to you."

Wetherill led his bay gelding away from the hitching post, swung himself into the saddle with the grace of a much younger man, and rode off to help Reading find his lost horse.

By the night of July 27 Reading was writing by campfire light once more. Kirkbride, Wetherill and the others who had arrived in the valley with Reading had parted his company reluctantly. They would go there own way now returning homeward down the Delaware as they had come. Reading himself had decided to travel east with some of the Yorkers on his way home. He wrote of his day:

"According to appointment Joseph Kirkbride and myself went to said Swartwoots in order to sign the instrument which after several debates pro and con was at last perfected." (Reading, 1915)

The job was done. As quickly as they had arrived, the various survey parties from Pennsylvania, West and East Jersey and New York left the Minisink valley. They went differing directions just as they had arrived, but not all by the same trails they had come on. In his journal Reading described his departure:

"Dr. Jonston, Mr. Willocks. Col. Hicks and myself designed to go by way of Goshen. We set forward with a guide from Mahackmech through the hills, through which we steered along a very blind path over very stony ground till we arrived at a branch of Hudson River known as wallakill, at an Indian

plantation in good fence, and well improved, raise wheat and horses, over which we led our horses by the side of a canoe, it being about 12 perch wide, with a great quantity of water, by the time we got over, it was almost dark but we stood along for Goshen, being about 3 miles distant, where we arrived about 9 of the clock and lodged at an ordinary called Michal Dunning. We were informed there were about 13 or 14 settlements in said town.[8]" (Reading, 1915)

Now he set his pen aside for a moment and wondered to himself what this work might mean for the people of the Minisink Valley. Each set of commissioners would return home now to file reports to their colonial superiors. The question was, how would those results be received.

The men who had worked so hard to set the important location on the river could not know that their conclusions would be rejected. Some of the officials who received their reports did not like the result. Much money hung in the balance, to be made or lost. The boundary questions would remain unsettled, for many years to come.

John Decker recovered from his fever. The Davids, Cole, Westfall, and Swartwood families went back to their trading, smithing, and farming. Life returned to a normal pace in the Minisink Valley. Relations with the local (Delaware) Munsi remained friendly for a couple decades more. But after that wet July, the Indians and the white settlers of the valley were always a bit edgy when they saw strangers or neighbors using compass and measuring chain.

---

[8] The word town used here denotes what in some states would now be called a Township. They often included a wide geographic territory encompassing rural areas and sometimes multiple villages.

Chapter 14: The Iroquois

*E*ighteen summers passed. Then in 1737, between the blooming of the dogwoods and the time of the mouse eared oaks, another delegation arrived in the Minisink Valley. These men were not here to study the heavens or survey the land. These were three Pennsylvania sheriffs, accompanied by two Iroquois sub-chiefs, all mounted horseback, and thirty Tuscarora braves, a-foot. They announced they were here to parley with the chiefs of the Munsi, "today".

It was a strange request. There had been no advance notice. It was unusual for such things to happen. Long held tradition called for a specific protocol usually requiring several days before any parley could begin. There had been no feasting, no preliminary greetings, no smoking of the sacred tobacco, no presents.

It was all very strange indeed, but the insulting proclamation had not been stated as a request. It was clearly a directive. And, the Iroquois were not a people one wished to annoy.

Immediately young men were sent off running into the forest. They must find the elders. Some of those leaders were far away from the village at this time. They must return.

Quickly the women of the tribe began preparing food. Despite their rudeness, these strangers must be fed. The Wolf Clan took great pride in their hospitality.

Bad behavior on the part of the strangers did not diminish the Munsi's responsibility to feed their guests. The people of the village performed their tribal duties with care but they were troubled. When they passed one another, outside earshot of their guests, they inquired quietly, one of another, what might be the purpose of this visit?

Jorris Davids had been out hunting that morning with Otter as they had done many mornings during the past two decades. On this day they returned to the village near eleven of the clock (had they owned a clock). Jorris noticed first the strange horses. Then, about the same moment, they both saw the strange men lounging outside one of the rectangular wigwams.

"Tuscarora," said Otter under his breath.

The two friends never hesitated in their stride as they attempted to appear neither fearful, nor especially interested. They passed-by only a few yards to the north of where the strangers stood.

They walked on toward the bark longhouse Otter now shared with his extended family. The two friends knew immediately, something important was about to happen. But neither knew exactly what. Whatever it was all about, the elders would have to decide how the village should respond. That decision had obviously not yet been made.

As they entered the longhouse Otter asked the women, who were busy cooking inside on the fire, about the strangers. Quickly he was told of the shameful slight, which had been suffered by his people, and of the pending talks. Then the women rushed out with dishes of food for their guests.

"Did you notice them braves watching us as we walked by?" Otter asked.

"Yeah, I noticed," said Jorris. "Those fella's do have a look don't they."

The Tuscarora were members of the Iroquois confederation and a fierce people. Each Iroquois tribe was a strong community by itself. But together they formed a union that had been unassailable, until the white men arrived just a couple generations ago. Even the whites feared the Iroquois, who fought only when they chose. But, when they decided around their council fires to fight, they fought with a ferocity and doggedness that always devastated their enemies.

Jorris Davids had grown to manhood knowing all this. He had heard the stories. He had also decided some time ago that he didn't much like these particular Indians.

But Jorris knew better than to get involved in business between Indians, especially if the Pennsylvania authorities were involved. He really didn't care much for Pennsylvania sheriffs either. In fact his experience with sheriffs, of any kind, had led him to believe that they were also to be avoided. But today, for some reason, he decided to stay and have a listen.

When the Elders came, everyone assembled near the central long-house. It was a big crowd. They shuffled in close to each other, hoping to hear what was said.

One of the Iroquois chiefs, stood to speak. He was a, middle aged, fierce looking man. The top half of his left ear was missing. A dark, wide, ugly, scar ran from the partial ear across the cheekbone of his broad face and terminated an inch or so under his left eye. Jorris watched the man stand and smile. But when he saw the smile, Jorris thought instantly, this was not a man who could be trusted.

"Brothers, we have met with the Quaker leaders in Philadelphia. The Pennsylvanians have told us you do not keep your bargains, which they make with you in good faith. This is not good. Therefore it has been decided by the Six–Nations, that the Delaware Indians must move beyond the mountains to the great river known as the Susquehanna. There you may share the land with your brother's the Shawnee. The Shawnee have already relocated themselves to that valley, to be far away from the white farmers. Our white brothers have purchased this land from you, in their Walking Treaty, to which you have agreed."

One of the Delaware elders attempted to rise and speak. But the other Iroquois chief leaped instead to his feet, interrupting, before the Munsi could begin.

"No!" said the Iroquois in a shrill voice. "The time for talk is over. The Delaware have not been true to their word. You are now like old women whining and crying for more beads, when you have been given all you need. You will move before the harvest moon. It would be good to go soon, so that you might establish your crops before that time comes, and survive the winter that will follow. Any who remain here, will not live to see the blackberry's bloom a second time. The Council Fires of the Six Nations have spoken. There is no more to say."

Abruptly the Iroquois and the Pennsylvania sheriffs rose. They stomped out of the meeting house. They mounted their horses, and rode out of the village heading south. The thirty Iroquois braves trotted behind them, their mocasined feet shuffling along the trail with no more sound than a breeze through the pines.

A strange quiet fell upon the village. The elders continued discussions in soft tones. These talks would, no doubt, continue into the night and likely for a few days more. The women elders would not be happy to leave their homes and fields behind. But they had no desire to see their men fight the Iroquois in a war they could not win.

Jorris said nothing as he and Otter walked to the river. They remained silent as they paddled to the New Jersey riverbank. When they beached the little bark, Jorris stumbled backward over a snag sticking up from the sand. Otter grabbed his friend, to prevent his fall. They laughed for an instant. Then Jorris asked.

"Will you go?"

"Yes," said Otter. "As a people we are not now, strong enough to do otherwise. The Iroquois and the English in Pennsylvania are brothers today."

He paused and stared at his friend for a long moment. The water lapped gently at the riverbank.

"It may not always be so. The Delaware Indians will move. But our memories are long. We will not forget our grand fathers—or the land, which has been our home. We will go, but we will remember our friends—and our enemies.

We will wait for a time when the Father-of-life no longer smiles upon the Iroquois, or their white brethren in Pennsylvania. Someday you will see us return.

The Delaware people are not old women, as the Iroquois say. When we come back, I will hope then—*not*, to find my friend Jorris standing with our enemy."

With that comment Otter pushed the little bark into the river and slipped aboard. Paddling swiftly the Indian headed across the water. Jorris watched after his friend for a long while until Otter had left his canoe high up, on the far bank, and walked into the village disappearing behind one of the bark wigwams.

Then Jorris Davids turned northeastward and trudged up the dark trail through the tall trees back toward his own cabin, at Kindiamong.

Chapter 15: The Christenings

"*O*ur most gracious heavenly father, we thank you for these children, who are brought here today by God fearing parents, to be christened in your holy church…" prayed the Dominie Wilhelm Mancius.

His prayer echoed less than it would later when the tiny stone church had a roof. For now, there were only squared beams, atop newly built stone walls, not yet even supporting rafters.

"We ask now a special blessing upon Solomon Davids, Jr, his wife Lea Decker and their new daughter Belietje; bless also their witnesses[9] Solomon Davids Sr. and his wife Belietje Quick…" said Mancius. (Multiple, Minisink Valley Reformed Dutch Church Records, 1915)

As he spoke, the breeze blew through the windowless, roofless structure rustling the hair on several uncovered heads bowed to the Dominie's words.

"We ask a special blessing upon Hendrich Kortrecht, his wife Margriet Dekker and their new daughter Lea; bless also their witnesses Johannes Dekker, and Lisabeth De Wit." (Multiple, Minisink Valley Reformed Dutch Church Records, 1915)

From the squirrel nest built high above, where the roof would later be, the view revealed a variety of scalps in the sanctuary below. There were a number of blond heads, several shades of brunet, some black, and of course a scattering, which were gray or becoming so.

Most of the bowed heads were still well covered in hair but a few had bald patches beginning to shine through. This was

---

[9] The choice of witnesses at a baby's christening was an important matter in the Dutch church. Witnesses were generally blood relatives or very close friends. To be a witness was akin to becoming a godfather or godmother accepting responsibilities for the spiritual well being of the child. It was an honor, not entered into lightly.

now the congregation at Minisink. The Munsi, who had previously lived on and near the island, had all moved west. White men now farmed the Indian fields of the island and on both sides of the big river.

"We ask now a special blessing upon Hendrich Kuikendal, his wife Lisabeth Cool and their new daughter Catryntje; bless also their witnesses David Cool and Leonora Westval" said the Dominie. (Multiple, Minisink Valley Reformed Dutch Church Records, 1915)

The reverend paused a moment to look out over his new congregation with a smile. He was a young man and he had dreamed for a long time of having his own congregation, where he could do Gods work. He was happy today, no matter how small the flock or how far removed into the wilderness it might be.

"We ask now a special blessing upon Gysbert Bogard, his wife Catharina Dekker and their new son Ezechiel, bless also their witnesses Hendrich Dekker, and Femmetje Dekker." (Multiple, Minisink Valley Reformed Dutch Church Records, 1915)

Local families had long petitioned the Reformed Dutch Congregation in Kingston for assistance. In answer to those prayers they had received Dominie Wilhelm Mancius as a missionary. Here he stood in his brown woolen breeches and his white shirt. The young minister had only recently arrived. Already they had a church sanctuary being built; and now they were christening their children here in the valley without the necessity of a three-day journey to far away Kingston.

"We ask a special blessing upon Petrus Dekker, his wife Magdalena Osterhout and their new daughter Catharina; bless also their witnesses Solomon Dekker and Femmetje Dekker." (Multiple, Minisink Valley Reformed Dutch Church Records, 1915)

As Mancius prayed, half a dozen crows flew in, landed in a nearby treetop and began to voice whatever it is crows always speak of when they gather.

The reverend looked up toward the tree, with an exasperated look on his round, blushing, face. A face bathed now in large wet beads of perspiration. He smiled. Then he began blotting his forehead and moist pink cheeks with a meager white handkerchief he held in his left hand, having just pulled it from under his wide leather belt. God's creatures were not going to spoil his day. He finished wiping his face, returned the kerchief to rest partially beneath his belt, and went on with the service.

"Finally we ask a special blessing upon Jacob Middag, his wife Sara Kuikendal and their new son Ephraim, bless also their witnesses Adrian Quick, and Lisabeth Westval." (Multiple, Minisink Valley Reformed Dutch Church Records, 1915)

After a short pause, annotated loudly by wretched, mischievous, noises from the tree, the reverend said in a determined voice, "This prayer we offer in the name of our Lord Jesus Christ, Amen".

The congregation raised their heads, and the missionary continued to speak above the ruckus being created by the birds:

"This concludes our service for today, this thirty-first day of May in the year of our Lord seventeen hundred and thirty eight. May God's blessings be upon each of you as you go forth and may he keep you safe until we gather together once again. God save King George."

"God save King George," responded the congregation in unison.

Quietly the people began to file from the church, which did not have yet, even a wooden door. The crows flew off, through a bright blue sky, deciding to continue their discussion elsewhere. They winged merrily away toward the nearby river cawing loudly to one another as they went.

All the new babies had fallen asleep during the ceremony. So the congregation now said their good-byes in whispered voices, heading out on horseback, in ox-carts and afoot, traveling differing directions to destinations, some nearby and others several miles distant.

While most of the congregation betook themselves toward home, the Davids family lingered. Lea ambled slowly toward the ancient maple where their big bay horse was tethered to the cart. Behind her walked her mother-in-law Belietje Quick Davids, humming a quiet tune, and carrying her namesake, the sleeping baby Belietje. Four-year-old Lea and the two-year-old Jacobus waddled along, following the women like two little ducklings, each toddler carrying a small piece of linen cloth in their right hand, sucking on its corner, and looking as if they might soon be asleep in the cart.

The Dominie had begun a conversation at the doorway of the church with thirty-year-old Solomon Jr. who was one year younger than the preacher but someone whom the minister had come to think he might need to know better.

Solomon Sr. stood with the younger men, his head down, listened patiently and working hard not to interrupt. It was difficult for him. He was not used to people seeking his son's opinions instead of his own. However, Solomon Jr. was already far better acquainted with the Dominie and the church than was he.

"How did a man as young as yourself acquire such a fine mill as you have?" asked Mancius.

Solomon Jr. thought for a moment, wondering about the minister's question. What was he really asking?

"A few years back, in 1730, Pa helped me buy the property from Samuel Green. Green had just purchased the Land himself, from a Munsi chief named Pennhorn, before the chief and his people moved west of the Fishkill. Green had a patent from East Jersey and we purchased from him in concert with Van Aken and Cole. We farmed the Indian fields at first. But working together we soon began clearing more acres."

Solomon glanced at his young wife and children, sitting with his mother under the maple:

"In '32' I married Lea. Her family has always lived just across on the other side of the Machackemack River from where my place is now. At least they've lived there as far back as I can remember. Then Lea and I began to build a place of our own. The mill came next. The Deckers have been a big help. It's a big family you know?"

"Yes I do know," responded the Dominie. "John Decker's family is beginning to spread all over this valley. I christened more than a few of the Decker Clan when I was still in Kingston; now I'm doing it here."

"Well, our families have always known one another, like most here in the valley," said Solomon. "Work always goes easier when it's done together. With friends and family, we were able to get the mill up and running in two years. That was the same year our oldest daughter, Lea, was born. (Multiple, Baptismal and Marriage Registers of the Old Dutch Church of Kingston, Ulster County, NY, 1891). Little Jacobus came next and now we have baby Belietje. We've been blessed".

"Is your New Jersey title to the land, good?" Wilhelm Asked.

"It is," said Solomon, "but it sounds like you might have been talking to Swartwood."

So this was the purpose of the Dominie's questions.

"It's true, I have spoken with Jacobus and others on the issue of the border," said Mancius. "There are strong feelings on both sides. I can see that it may be difficult for us to keep peace among our congregation here."

"But when we worship we must be one people. God expects us to love even our enemy," said the missionary as he smiled and winked at Solomon.

"Well Reverend, we will just have to try, but this feud has been going on for a lot of years. Mostly the Swartwoods and the Westbrooks are Yorkers and mostly the Westfalls are New Jersey men. Other families are split, depending on how and when they bought their land."

"It's been near 20 years since the station point was set up near Coshecton. We were here then, even if others weren't. They told us it was resolved back then."

Solomon drew a long thoughtful breath and looked Mancius straight in the eyes.

"But it weren't."

"Still today the Royal Governors won't settle the issue for certain. The longer it goes undecided the more frustrated people around here become. None of us want to work a lifetime developing a homestead or a mill, and then give it up, without a fight, because some lawyer tells us we did not have the right to purchase, or that we bought it from the wrong folks.

Nobody wants to pay taxes on the same property in two different colonies. And by-golly none of us want to be required to serve in two different militias. It's a thorny issue and that's for sure!"

"Yes, I see," said Mancius looking down at the ground. Then he suddenly looked up brightly. "Well, maybe now that the Savages across the river have moved further west, there will be plenty of land for all."

"I'll see to the horse!" said Solomon Sr., and he turned, tramping away toward the animal tethered to the cart under the tree.

"Reverend, that's something else folks around here don't agree on much," said Solomon Jr.

The two men moved off the steps and sauntered a few paces toward the family near the horse and cart. Solomon paused, listening to the scream of a hawk off somewhere in the distance.

"Some of us grew up living real close with the Munsi People. They sold us their land on this side of the river and they traded with us for many years, when we needed their furs. They still trade with some of us. We hunted and fished together and lived as good neighbors should."

Solomon looked off toward the west for a moment. Billowy, white clouds hung in a blue sky over the Pocono. An Eagle rode the thermals.

"Now more white men are coming from up North and even through the mountains from the East. Palatine Germans are coming from the south—from Philadelphia, and over Birks county way. They're settling now in numbers, just across the Kitatinny Ridge, there, in the valley of the Paulins-kill."

"A couple years back the Pennsylvanians saw an opportunity to profit. They talked the Munsi into selling some of their land south of here, on the west side of the big river. They called it their 'Walking Treaty'. It was supposed to be land as far as a man could walk north in a day and then back to the river.

The Indians thought that meant back due east to the river. But the Pennsylvanians ran the line northeast taking in far more land, including the most important and sacred Munsi land, that land which is on the Pennsylvania side of the river, opposite our valley here.

The Munsi knew they had been tricked and refused to move. Then, at the request of the Pennsylvanians, the Iroquois forced the Munsi out, all the way to the Susquehanna. It was some fast talking, but it weren't right."

The minister began to twist his face into what Solomon recognized as his thoughtful pose. Solomon knew he had the man struggling with this moral dilemma.

Solomon had strong feelings on this issue. But he knew there were others in the reverends congregation, who saw the treaty much differently. He wondered if their new minister would ever be able to understand his point of view. Most people, who had not grown up here, living their lives among the Munsi, did not seem to understand, or care to try. They wanted cheap land. They did not seem to mind, that the previous owners had not really wanted to sell it.

Pennsylvania encouraged settlement by offering cheap land prices. Some folks just paid the money and moved across the river. At least over there they didn't have to worry about the feud between New York and the Jerseys.

This struggle over who owned the land was indeed a very thorny issue. The Munsi would likely never get their land back, without a fight. But Solomon wondered if he could ever make the missionary understand why that was so wrong.

"Now that the Munsi have moved to the Susquehanna, newcomers, and some of their old neighbors too, see a new opportunity to profit. They are moving onto the Indian lands, even further west. They are moving now, toward the Munsis' new home. It may be legal, but that don't always make it right. Does it?" asked Solomon.

"Well I don't know," said the minister, as he rubbed his chin and watched a large red ant climbing onto his boot toe. "I guess that would be the King's business, not the business of the Church. But I see your point."

The ant climbed back off his boot. He raised his head slowly, with a smile.

"I believe Solomon, that you are a man who concerns himself with what is right—and good. I hope we can find ways to work together. The church and the community will need men like you if we're to prosper. It 's hard country. We'll need to work together if we're to have peace."

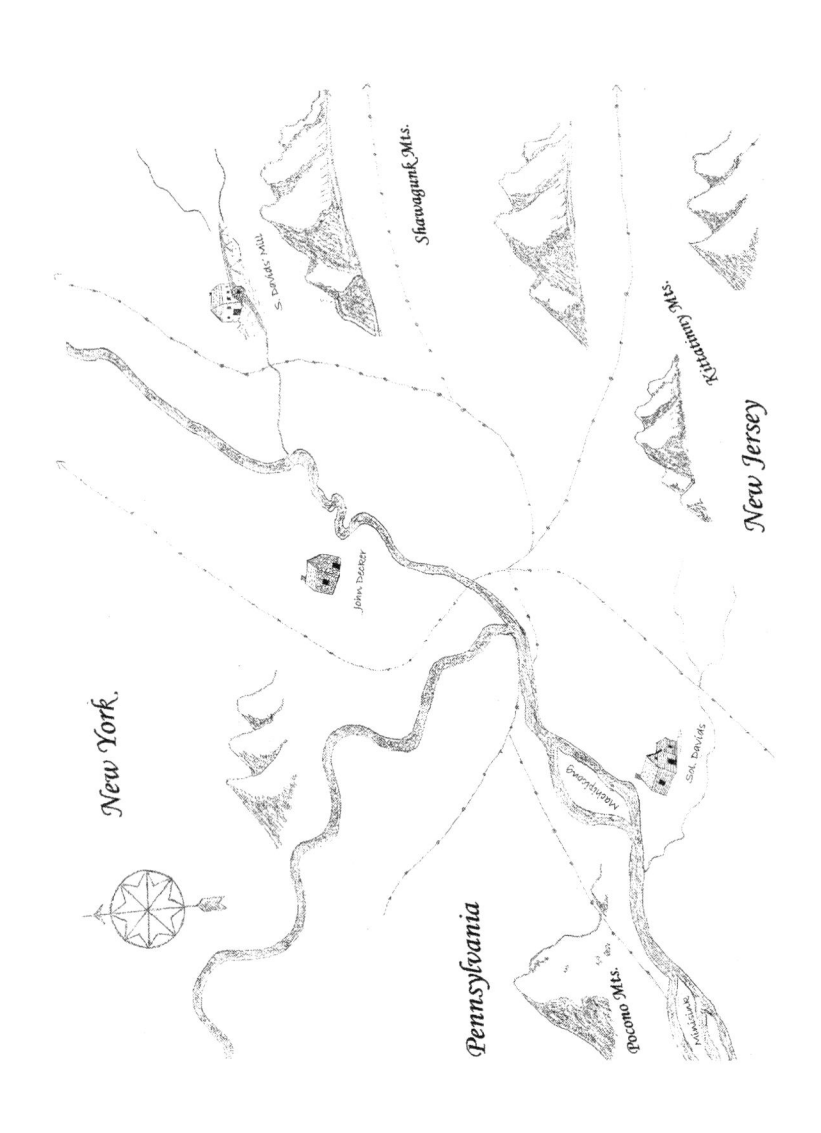

Chapter 16: The Dutch Church with a Roof

Two years and almost a month, after baby Belietje had been christened in the new Reformed Dutch Church at Minisink, the Davids family was back in the stone structure, with a new child. The service was drawing toward its close and the minister began his now familiar prayer for concluding such occasions.

"Our most gracious heavenly father, we thank you today for these children brought here by god fearing parents, to be christened in your holy church. We ask a special blessing on Solomon Davids, Jr, his wife Lea Decker and their new son Daniel; bless also their witnesses, Daniel Kuikendal and Lisabeth Van Aaken." (Multiple, Minisink Valley Reformed Dutch Church Records, 1915)

The minister's words echoed a little more now that the sanctuary had a roof. It was June and the plank window shutters and front doors were open wide, encouraging in any gentle, cooling breeze, which might happen along on such a warm day. But the air remained heavy and still.

"We ask a special blessing upon Jacobus Dekker, his wife Neeltje Ditsoort and their new daughter, Leatje; bless also their witnesses Solomon Davids, Jr and Lea Decker. (Multiple, Minisink Valley Reformed Dutch Church Records, 1915)

The missionary and the Davids family had become well acquainted in the past two years. Both men continued to straddle the fence regarding the local border dispute. Each in his own way worked to keep peace among their neighbors.

But, as more acres were cleared and farmsteads expanded, new conflicts seemed to sprout with the crops. Colonial leaders in neither Albany nor Elizabethtown seemed interested, willing or able to settle the problem.

"We ask a special blessing upon Johannes Dekker, his wife Lana Quick and their new son Wilhelmus; bless also their witnesses William Dietsoort and Sara Dekker." (Multiple, Minisink Valley Reformed Dutch Church Records, 1915)

As the minister paused, a black and white woodpecker the size of a crow, with red head and shoulders, landed on a dead limb in a tree just outside the church window. The bird cocked his head to one side and then to the other as if looking for just the right spot. Then he began drumming on the wood. The limb where the bird began prospecting for insects was quite hollow and with each strike it reverberated now, like a great drum, creating quite a racket. But, Mancius had become accustomed to having nature's accompaniments here in the valley. He smiled more to himself that the congregation.

"This concludes our service for today," said Mancius. "May God bless you and keep you and may God save King George."

"God Save King George!" responded the crowd.

Almost instantly, six-year-old Lea, four-year-old Jacobus and two-year-old Belietje shot out the door, their moccasined little feet slapping the ground as they raced happily toward the horse tethered to the cart under the maple. The congregation followed, at a more civilized pace, speaking of the services but also about the raid into the valley only two weeks before:

"Well, Petrus … McKay[10] and his boys had better be careful next time they come over that pass, to collect taxes. Folks are fed up, with being dragged to Goshen…."

"Thats right, Aaron … McKay may need those hundred-fifty men he claims will back him…."

"Congratulations Lea, I believe Daniel looks just like Belietje when she was a baby…."

Suddenly all three of the newly christened babies began to cry. Everyone else—grown men as well as women—began

---

[10] Colonel of the Orange County New York militia at this time.

then, to laugh, or coo, or speak in strange tiny voices, appealing to the infants. But the babies cried all the louder.

Solomon and Reverend Mancius stood on the church-steps lost in their own private conversation.

"Well reverend what do you think?"

The missionary had just finished reading a letter addressed to Solomon and other New Jersey Officials from Governor Morris[11] in Elizabethtown. Solomon had handed Mancius the letter after the service ended.

"Looks like he is straddling a fence of his own Sol. He wants to be careful. But he did share your report with the council instead of just ignoring it. That's something."

"Yeah it's something Reverend, but what do you think of their direction?"

"Well, it's like most resolutions from the council. It orders you and officers like you in two directions at once. That way, regardless of what happens, the council themselves have their reputations protected. Listen to this part."

The minister read a few words to himself to find his place, then read aloud the Governors words:

"I have received a letter from Solomon Davids Esq., one of the Justices of the peace for the county of Morris, Informing me that a number of persons Inhabitants in the Province Of New York have, in a disorderly and tumultuous manner, entered into the County of Morris in this province of New Jersie, and forcibly have taken and carried several of the inhabitants thereof to prison in the province of New York." (Morris, 1852)

---

[11] Lewis Morris, Royal Governor of the province of New Jersey 1738-1746.

The minister lowered the letter and looked at Solomon with a raised brow.

"So we know he got your report and he seems to understand what's happening. He goes on to explain why it should not be happening. But then, the council gets involved. And that's when you get your orders. Listen to this last part." Again he read from the letter:

"The board gave it as their unanimous opinion that, his Excellency should direct the magistrates in the said County of Morris to avoid as much as possible all strife & contention with the inhabitants of the province of New York, and to do their duty in preserving the peace and protecting the Inhabitants of the said county of Morris from any insults that may be offered them." (Morris, 1852)

"Well good luck, Sol. They want you to defend the people from all insult, but be sure not to upset or offend those who are dragging them off to another colony, where they must post bond to stay out of Jail. That would be hard enough. But then the governor adds his own little twist."

Once more Mancius read from the letter:

"This I require to be done, & hope it will be duly performed with a proper & suitable prudence & becoming resolution." (Morris, 1852)

Mancius snickered. "Be prudent but resolute. What exactly does that mean?"

"Pardon me Sol, but that sounds like he wants you to keep the trouble makers out of New Jersey, but he won't be able to back you up, if any of the Kings subjects from New York get hurt while your doing it."

Mancius looked over toward Solomon's family who were waiting near the horse and cart. He drew a contemplative breath and turned back to Solomon.

"I'll contact the church fathers in Kingston again and do what I can for you. Of course the Church Fathers will want to see things from the New York side and a good part of our congregation here will see it that way as well. But I see the excesses coming at you from Goshen. We both know, most people just pick the side they stand to gain from. It's up to the Royal Governors to resolve this issue and settle that boundary. Until they do my friend, my advice to you … is to be, *very careful*.

Chapter 17: Jaol

$\mathcal{L}$ife continued in the valley. Old people died, young people married and more babies were born. Winters were snowy and summers hot. Three years passed after Governor Morris's letter directing Solomon Jr. to keep troublemakers out of the Minisink. The Van Akens built a new barn with the help of their neighbors. It was a small bank barn built of stone. Solomon Jr. cleared another nine acres near the river. A few new families moved into the area. But the border question was still not settled.

As Mancius had suggested, Solomon had tried to be careful. But somehow he had been arrested by the Orange County Sherriff, and found himself now in the Orange County Jaol (Jail).

It was dark inside the single room jaol. The log walls, of square hewn oak, were chinked securely between, with a hard mixture of dried clay and straw. There were no windows. The only light entering was from a crack around the plank door, and a tiny twelve inch square hole, in the top quarter of that door, where the jailer sometimes handed in a cup of water, from a nearby well, or some thin porridge from the jaol's meager rations.

It was not a pleasant place and Solomon, today, was not a happy man. At this moment, he was trying hard to hear the discussion in the room above him. It was not going well.

He could hear a few horse flies buzzing loudly inside his cell; occasionally he heard the sudden clomp of a heavy hoof, or the swish of a tail, as the horses fought their own battle with the flies just outside, at the hitching rail in front.

The wide oak floorboards above his head sifted sand down, whenever anyone walked across the upper room and he could certainly hear clearly, when a chair or bench skittered, scraped, or slid across the floor. But nothing being said, in the room above, reached his ear in more than a drone of mumbled, indistinguishable communication.

At approximately eleven of the clock, scowling at the experience he had just endured, Jorris Davids emerged from the Orange County courtroom in Goshen. He squinted as he came out into the brighter light and adjusted his hat. In quick steps he descended the steep, outside, wooden, stairway, attached alongside the two-story log building. The bottom room below the court was the Jail.

A tired looking jailor lumbered along, a few steps behind Jorris. Clearly, he was in no particular hurry. He descended the steps slowly and shuffled around the building.

Jorris stood in front of the structure, facing a dusty street. He was rubbing the back of his stiff neck and waiting impatiently, beside the heavy plank door. No other activity was in sight, except for two little barefoot boys scudding up the street, rolling an empty wooden keg before them, and followed by a small white dog, barking and scampering along with a happily wagging tail.

Jorris stared at the jailor indignantly. The fellow had the slack hungry look of a man who seldom had enough to eat but who could just never quite summon enough energy, on his own, to go hunt. Jorris had seen others like him. They usually stayed close to towns like Goshen each winter hoping they would not be allowed to starve.

The man gazed back at Jorris, with a dim-witted smirk. But he did not get in a hurry. He had all day.

The Jailor carried three large keys on a metal ring. Now he held them out, eye level, in front of himself. Carefully and very deliberately he selected one of the keys, as if it were the biggest decision he might make in a week. He inserted the key into a large iron lock, turned it with a loud clank, and slowly swung open the thick plank door, to the sound of creaking wooden hinges.

Immediately, Solomon Davids, Jr stepped into the full morning light for the first time in four days. He put on his hat, blinked a couple times and smiled at his brother. Jorris turned and strode a few steps to their waiting horses, tied to a post in front of the jail.

Nothing was said. Nothing needed to be said. Both men mounted and turned their horses west along the road heading out toward Minisink. Neither brother looked back as they rode away.

A couple miles out of town they came to a ford on the Wallkill. The water today was not deep and their horses got over easily without a swim. As the animals lunged up the muddy west bank, two armed riders sprang from the brush, on either side of the trail, smiling down upon them.

"Morning Sol," said one of the men.

"Morning Josias, morning Willem," returned Solomon.

The man called Willem handed Solomon a musket, which he held in his hand and pulled up another he had hung by a leather strap from his saddle.

"They're loaded and primed," he told Solomon.

Together the four men continued to ride up the trail. Quickly they covered another quarter mile and were topping a low ridge, when two more riders emerged from the woods.

"Morning Dirk—Aaron—how are you boys today?" said Solomon.

Then there were six riders traveling up slope toward the mountains. Five minutes further along, the trail intersected a faint path, which headed off to the left following a small stream, which meandered its way back toward the Wall-kill. Here, two more mounted and armed men, appeared out of the brush as the group approached. Each of the new men nodded toward Solomon who greeted them:

"Morning Jury—morning Andries."

The two fell in with the others and together they continued their slow, plodding, climb up the east slope of the Shawagunk Mountains.

As the rocky trail narrowed, the horses fell in behind one another and Solomon turned back, smiling at his brother:

"Were you expecting trouble today?"

"Not taking chances anymore," answered Jorris.

"Figured if anyone followed the two of us from town, they might forget to bring enough help to take on eight."

"You don't have any more surprises up ahead do you?"

"Nope, figured eight were enough, besides it's wheat harvest and everybody else was busy."

After sundown the next day, Solomon and his escort rode back into the Minisink. When they reached the intersection where the trail from Goshen, and Pennhorn road came together, they were too tired for long goodbyes. The horses simply drifted apart each carrying their rider toward his own barn. Most of the men were half asleep in the saddle—some more than half.

Jorris turned his horse right, down Pennhorn road, expecting to spend the night at Solomon's place. A mile later they arrived to find the Davids' house with the door open and lit by candlelight. Lea and the children were waiting.

Six-year-old Belietje saw the riders first. Squealing: "Papa!" She raced across the yard to greet her father as he dismounted his horse. Quickly Solomon scooped her up and gave her a big hug as he did for ten-year-old Lea, eight-year-old Jacobus and three-year-old Daniel each in turn as they came running up. Wife, Lea was last to approach as she came along accompanied by Reverend Fryenmoet.

Last Spring Reverend Fryenmoet had replaced Rev. Mancius at the Dutch church. He was thinner and rougher in his manner, but he had been prepared by his predecessor and was getting to know the local congregation quite well.

After her hug, Lea smiled at Solomon and said, "The Reverend came by to see if he might be of any help. Little Daniel has been telling him all evening, that Uncle Jorris was gone to Goshen[12] to get his Pa out of the Jail-house. He doesn't understand."

"Well that makes two of us," said Solomon.

"They said they arrested me for performing my duties to New Jersey. But I also try hard to meet my responsibilities to New York. This is getting to be a tough fence to straddle, Reverend."

The minister smiled. Solomon went on.

"I guess as long as folks here in the valley keep electing me I will do my best. It's up to the governors to settle this border question, not me. I expect the Jersies will find some excuse to put me in jail next. There are hot heads on both sides and none of them like me much."

"Solomon, you always do your best," said the Reverend Fryenmoet.

"I try reverend. I really do. Most people just want us to keep a lid on the trouble before it boils over. And we might be able to do that, if the boys from Goshen would stay on their own side of the mountain and mind their own business."

"Well I'll see what I can do, to help you Sol. I'll write the church fathers and see if they will send another letter on your behalf to the governor in Albany. They will want to be careful about the politics. But our Church is expanding now, deep into New Jersey with the new group down at Walpack and then there's the church on into Pennsylvania, down at Lower Smithfield. We all want to keep that lid on the trouble. Most of the people here trust you and need for you to do that job. Reverend Mancius understood all that and so do I."

He placed his hand lightly on Solomon's shoulder and squeezed:

"But be careful. Politics is a strange, and sometimes dangerous business."

---

[12] Goshen was the county seat for Orange County New York.

"Some people can get downright mean, when they think you are standing between them and a quick profit. Or if they think someone is about to take something from them. It's human nature, I guess."

"God help us. People can always convince themselves that what they want to do, is also somehow the right thing to be done. Sometimes it is. But more often, unfortunately, there is usually right and wrong, good and bad on both sides. That's why it is so dangerous for people like you Solomon—people caught in the middle. It's hard to keep the hot heads from dragging the good folks into a war."

The minister frowned.

"And then there are always those 'owned by the devil'!"

"These men are consumed by evil. They're always eager to stir folks up to a war, hoping for the chance to plunder what they themselves have not been able to earn. As you like to say, it's a thorny problem."

" Just be-careful Solomon that you don't get cut too badly, by those thorns."

"Well it's not how it ought to be, Reverend."

"No… But it's the way things are. We have to take the world the way we find it Solomon, until we have the time to make it better. Bide your time and be careful."

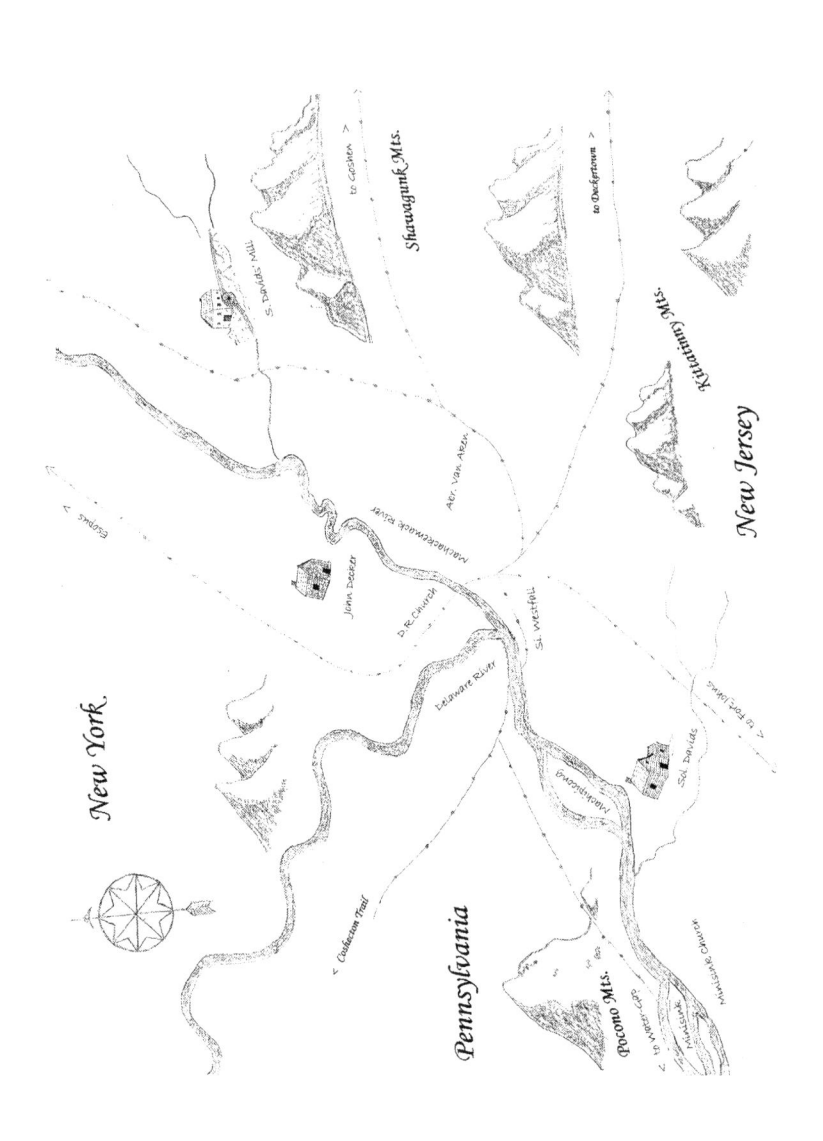

Chapter 18: Home at the Mill

Seven years passed and little changed in the Minisink Valley except that the families grew ever larger and the need for more land became even more apparent.

Something rustled the leaves just now, a few yards up slope on the far bank, as thirteen- year-old Belietje Davids slipped her bare foot into the cool water of the little stream.

"Likely it's a ground squirrel," she thought.

But she knew it could be one of those little salamanders or a land turtle or even a snake. Sometimes they would move the leaves and make a noise like this, but usually it was a ground squirrel.

Today was a hot quiet day, during barley harvest. Mr. Van Aken was in the mill with Pa. He had already brought in a small amount of new grain to be ground. Wheat harvest was yet a ways off and any kind of flour was scarce this time of year.

Belietje stepped her other foot into the little rocky stream being careful to keep her dress pulled slightly higher to stay out of the water. Ma did not like to see the hem of her dress wet. Besides, Ma said, she was getting to be a woman now and needed to start behaving like one. That meant tending more to chores needing done, and less to wading in streams.

Belietje had always loved the little kill that ran through their farmstead. In hot weather, like today, she particularly enjoyed it here, behind the mill.

It was here that the wooden mill-sluice directed water from above, out onto the big wheel. The water-wheel boxes filled and the added weight causing the wheel to move round, turning the millstones inside and grinding the grain.

In the shade under the sluice there was always water dripping and a soft green carpet of mosses growing. The big wheel had a comforting sound. It creaked and thumped slowly to the constant accompaniment of the splashing water, which after completing its work spilled out into the tailrace and flowed on toward the Machackemack River.

Belietje had been spinning wool in the warm house since before breakfast. A few minutes ago her sister Lea had come to take a turn at the spinning wheel. Lea had just returned from taking the noon meal of fried ham to Jacobus and Daniel. The boys were hoeing corn in the big field near the river. They would not be home till dusk.

Belietje knew she could not be long at the stream. She was needed to help Ma pull weeds, in the garden. There was always more than enough work for everyone.

Although she did not feel like a full-grown woman today, she knew she was no longer a child. She intended to do her share of the work. She would give no-one reason to call her lazy. But for the moment she needed a short respite here, before reporting to the hot sun of the two-acre garden.

The sounds in the leaves had been intermittent but she thought she could hear it again just now. She knew she heard crows cawing down by the river. They had probably found an old owl asleep in a tree and they were calling in reinforcements for the battle. She looked across the fields but couldn't see a single bird. She knew they were there though. She imagined them wheeling in short flight patterns around the unfortunate bird they had decided to torment.

As she listened she began to wonder what life might be like for her, when she married and left home to start a family of her own. She was not so anxious to do such a thing, as some girls she knew. She enjoyed her present family too much.

Her pa was a good man and he had a successful mill. Her grandfather Decker's farm was just across the Mackhackemack River. Family and friends were everywhere she seemed to look. There always had been enough food and a warm fire, even in the hardest winters. She knew that every farm in the valley was not so fortunate.

Her Family had lived in the area since before her ma and pa were born. They had built a comfortable life, even if it were not always an easy one. Belietje had grown up hearing stories of the struggle. Blizzards and floods, good crops and bad, peace times and wars were what the people remembered and how they marked time in their lives.

In her own short life she had always known of the border conflict. She knew people on both sides of that issue and she had seen the frustration grow. She remembered when her Pa had been arrested and put in the Goshen Jail. But most days people went about their lives being cordial to one-another, at least at church, or the Mill, or in the Blacksmith shop.

The same year her Pa was put in the jail he was honored a few months later by the Royal Justices in Kingston. They appointed him to represent their interest, in the building of the Church Sanctuary at Machackemack. That stone building now stood a mile and half south of grandfather Decker's house on the west side of the river. Her little brother Joel had been christened there that same year and baby Jonas the next. (Multiple, Minisink Valley Reformed Dutch Church Records, 1915)

The year after Jonas was christened Ma convinced Pa not to be elected constable. So the neighbors elected Uncle Jorris. But he wasn't suited to that much talk.

So the next year, when her sister Catherine had been born Pa and his friend Mathew Brink were elected to share the duties. (Multiple, Record of Minutes, Surveys, Stock Marks and Business Conducted by Precincts of Minisink and Motague 1737-1782, 1915) Ma was happier having two constables in the precinct, but she still wished Pa wasn't one of them.

Two years later she got her wish. When Ma was pregnant with baby Elizabeth the neighbors elected the Westfall boys to be constables in the Minisink Precinct. At first Pa was upset. He said ma had asked her family to vote for the Westfalls and they did.

Pa liked the Westfall brothers and thought they would be fair. Other folks didn't seem so sure. But the Westfall brothers did the job for the next few years anyhow.

Now, here it was almost 1750, the beginning of a new decade. Baby Petrus had just been birthed and the Davids family would now have one more member, with which to share the work. Baby Petrus was doing fine but the Westfall boys were having trouble with the neighbors. Some folks who lived out on the trail toward Decker-Town were feuding about hogs, or some-such-thing. Belietje just didn't understand. People were beginning to talk about electing her Pa constable again. Ma sure wasn't happy about that.

It was a ground squirrel she had heard. Finally, he finished rutting in the leaves and came out to sit on a mossy rock. The squirrel watched the girl step out of the water and slip on her moccasins. He barked sharply, after her, twice, as she walked out into the hot sunshine. But Belietje Davids, skipped away toward the garden, with the smile of a girl who knew her place in the world and was happy in it.

Chapter 19: March 1750

Thunder rumbled over the Poconos. Forty-year-old Solomon Davids, Jr stepped out from the doorway of his gristmill.[13] He looked west over the Machackemack River. Low rolling dark clouds, were being highlighted intermittently by flashes of purple and orange slashing through the wet gray sky.

It had been over thirty years since the rainy July of 1719. Solomon had once again found himself elected constable of Minisink Precinct. (Multiple, Record of Minutes, Surveys, Stock Marks and Business Conducted by Precincts of Minisink and Motague 1737-1782, 1915) The border between New Jersey and New York was still not settled. In fact folks were arguing about it more than ever.

It seemed that 'wet' July was long ago, but then again like it was just yesterday. So much had happened and yet other things had hardly changed. A few more families had moved into the valley. Westbrook, Brink, Van-Etten, Middag, and Rosenkrans were all common names now. Still there were fewer than 50 families spread along 30 miles of flat land beside the Machackemach and Fishkill Rivers and now there were four small Dutch Reformed church-houses built in the valley. All of them sharing the one traveling minister.

New York officials from Orange County collected taxes here and expected men from the valley to serve in their militia. There was talk of forming another New Jersey county from northwestern parts of Morris County just as Morris County had once been formed from parts of the old Hunterdon County. This new unit of government would likely have its courthouse also on the east side of the Kittatinny Mountains. Certainly it would have the same claims on territory,

---

[13] This would be the mill located on Pennhorn Road which some twenty-nine years later would be burned to the ground during a raid into the valley led By Joseph Brant an Iroquois Chief loyal to the British during the American Revolution. But that is a later story.

overlapping or preceding Orange County claims—all depending upon your perspective.

For year's men outside the valley from both New Jersey and New York had conducted raids into the Minisink to steel crops or collect taxes depending again upon your point of view. Now-days rumors abounded and Solomon could see no end to the trouble. To many powerful interests outside the valley still stood to lose money.

Solomon Jr. agreed with his father that Kendiamong was clearly in New Jersey. His brother Jorris and his growing family lived now in a new cabin on land from part of their original thousand-acre patent. Solomon Jr.'s sentiments were clear with regard to that property.

His, own mill-property and the Decker farm of his in-laws was another matter. Recent speculations in the community seemed to lean toward land above the Machackamech branch being or becoming a part of Orange County, New York. Solomon Jr. had always tried to hedge his bets in regard to that issue.

"Shoot," he told himself, "half my customers see themselves as Yorkers and the other half are New Jersey men. How am I to know what is right when even at church the two sides bicker."

Today Solomon stood outside his mill watching the coming storm and pondering the border problem. Suddenly he was aware of thundering hooves on soft earth. He glanced northward up Pennhorn Road to see two large, dark-chestnut horses approaching at a dead run, side by side like a runaway matched team without a wagon. Their riders, tall lanky men, were hunched over and stretching forward over the horses necks as if to see whose nose would cross the finish line first—man or steed.

The stride of the big chargers was long and they covered the distance quickly. First one and then the other seemed to gain the advantage with both riders urging their mount on with an occasional slap of a leather strap. Soon they past the little dip in the road and thundered up the hill. The riders drew rein only when they passed the barn. When they pulled up, the horses responded by skidding to a halt in front of the mill, tossing their heads high, snorting and pulling deep, to catch their wind.

The riders like the horses were a matched pair in appearance and build, making allowances for the gray hair and weathered hide on the one. Not only did they look alike but they rode with a similar, simple grace and possessed the identical fun loving smile displayed now as they calmed their mounts, with soothing tones and firm pats to the side of the neck, in fond appreciation and admiration, for all the effort just expended.

When the horses settled a bit, the two men dismounted, in unison, the balls of their moccasined feet, hitting the earth with an athletic spring, at almost the exact same moment.

"How you doin boys?" said Solomon.

The older of the riders answered, "Thought we might sit out the storm with you Solomon, if that be alright."

Solomon had known Tom Quick all his life, and Tom Quick Jr. since the boy had been born almost sixteen, no—seventeen years ago. They were family. Both had already tied their horses and were busy tossing stirrups over cannels, and untying leather straps, before Solomon could even answer: "Sure thing—come on in."

Quickly the men yanked the saddles and carried them inside the mill; young Tom emerging immediately to hustle away, leading the horses to the coral near the barn, opening the gate and turning them in. Then he trotted himself back, up the steps, and inside the mill.

Last fall's leaves, dark and discolored, suddenly began to blow again, across the valley, having just recently emerged from the winter snow. The air was heavy and foretold the coming rain. Huge wet drops slapped the left side of Solomon's face now, as he stepped inside, pulling the heavy wooden door closed behind him, with a thump.

An hour passed. The rain stopped but the wind, outside, blew colder. Inside, the three men sat, smoking clay pipes, before a burning fire in the stone fireplace. Flame shadows danced on the dimly lit stone walls. Except for the firelight, the mill was dark.

Today, like all days, the place smelled of corn, wheat, and other grain. Hemp sacks hung all about, and a small stack of oak firewood stood along an inside wall. The fire was warm. Blue tobacco smoke curled lazily in the air between the long stemmed pipes and the fireplace flue. It was a good place to be, on such a cold, wet day.

It was quiet. No one had spoken for some time.

"Have you seen any Sheriffs lately?" asked the old man.

"Not lately" answered Solomon, slowly drawing on his pipe. Then, after a long pause he added: "Not from Jersey or York."

Silence settled again, except for the roof creaking in the wind. The younger Tom had stopped smoking and was dozing in his chair. Another five minutes passed and old Tom asked:

"You ever see Twisted-stalk, or Red-corn, or any of the old boys from Minisink anymore?"

"Not fer' a couple years. The Susquehanna is a distance; and I guess they don't care to come fer visits!" Solomon answered.

The fire crackled. Suddenly a burning log shifted sending a broken wavering line of hot cherry-red sparks shooting up the flue. The men stared into the flame and basked for the moment in its warmth.

"Well they got no call to be mad at us. We didn't tell 'em to go!" The old man asserted. He shifted himself in the chair turning his profile toward the flames to toast his right side. "It was the Iroquois and that greedy Board of Property down in Philadelphia who cooked up that Walking Treaty trouble."

"Well it weren't right!" said Solomon.

"No it weren't!" answered the old man. "But that was over ten year ago, they might as well get over it. People got to make a livin'—and to do that they got to have good land."

The quiet returned between them. Outside the wind blew harder drawing the sparks and the smoke up the flue with a friendly roar. The two sat quietly again staring into the fire. The back of Solomon's tongue grew hot. He took the pipe from his mouth and popped its bowl against the palm of his hand, dumping the ash onto the stones in front of the fire. He took a slow breath, got up and started poking at the fire with a charred stick. Then he added a new oak log to the coals.

"Trouble is Tom, now the Connecticut farmers are buying supplies at Dupui's, down at Shawnee, and pushing way on into Pennsylvania. They're knocking on the door, of the Delaware Nation all over again—you know that ain't right!"

Old Tom watched the yellow flames lick slowly at the fresh log and thought about Solomon's last comment for another minute, before responding:

"Well no it aint! But what have we got to do with that! The Pennsylvania sheriffs tried to stop them fools from moving' onto Indian lands. They burned them out—didn't they, a little while back—killin' more than just a few as I recall."

"Still I hear they keep on comin', sayin' it's their right, by the Kings Charter. I don't know the truth of it all, but Dupui has been told now, to stop sellin' to em'.

It may not be right for the Munsi, but it ain't our fault, and it ain't our concern."

Solomon watched the yellow flames rise up to overspread the fresh log he had placed on the fire.

"Well you're probably right." he said. He thought to himself for another moment. "Old Tom is kin after-all. He was one of the first to buy property from Pa at Kendiamong, before he gave it up, to moved across the Fishkill, building a mill on the Pennsylvania side. I shouldn't forget he advised me on the buildin' of this very mill we're a-sittin' in. He's just doing what he thinks he has to do, to keep his family fed. There's no need to get his dander up."

Solomon sighed. "Tom—I'm just a-feared that all this scrapping around over the land, is goin to lead to some real trouble one of these days."

The old man turned in his chair to face his friend. His manner softened and his gray eyes sparkled a bit. He assumed a kindly face and spoke slowly.

"Solomon, you're a good man; but you worry too much!"

Suddenly old Tom stood, kicking his son's boot lightly.

"Wake up boy! We got to get home afore dark."

In a couple minutes the two travelers were saddled up and mounted.

As he sat his horse, old Tom hesitated for a moment and then said, "Solomon, 'stead of worrying so much about your old Munsi friends, you need to be mindin' this trouble 'tween the Yorkers and Jersies. Things is gettin' mighty heated up. You might want to cool your opinions some, and watch your back. There's been talk—that's all I'm goin' to say."

The old man paused and looked sharply off toward the north.

"But one more thing." He lowered his voice and leaned down over the saddle. "Watch out for your cousin, Petrus Quick. I know he is blood kin, but he has married into the Swartwood clan and he never did like you much, since you both was boys—but that's all I'm a sayin'."

The two men reined their horses toward Pennhorn road. Young Tom noticed all the rattle- snake hides hanging on Solomon's near-by barn.

"Seen any snakes lately?" he called back.

"Not lately!" Solomon shouted.

The two Quick's chuckled, as they trotted their horses off, toward the Mill-Ford and Pennsylvania.

Chapter 20: Night Ride

It was a frosty clear night, late in October 1751. Long after the sun had set, a large full moon lit up the sky to the east and rose over the Kittatinny Ridge flooding the valley with its' silvery glow. Suddenly, a saddled but rider-less horse trotted past the door of the Davids' house, stopping to drink at the water trough between the mill and the barn. Sixteen-year-old Jacobus emerged from inside and trotted himself over to the horse, the other children soon peering out the doorway after him.

"Who is it Jakey?" asked Belietje from inside.

"It's Pa's horse, Old Red," came his answer, along with the sudden realization that something was bad wrong.

Instantly, Ma appeared at the door. Beleitje with her older sister Lea came hurrying across the yard to see for themselves.

"Stay in the house!" Ma said to the other children and then she added, "Daniel get the musket down from the rack. Now!"

Jacobus was feeling with his hands all over the horse's neck and saddle as the girls approached. He turned toward them and said, "Mount up Beletie!"

Quickly he joined the fingers of both his hands together into an improvised stirrup and bent down low. Beleitje stepped her bare left foot into his hands and was tossed by her brother up into the saddle, in one fluid motion, like it had been done a thousand times before.

"Don't put that girl on a horse! She can't ride." Yelled Ma from the cabin.

"Hush Ma!" Jacobus shouted back: "She rides better than anyone in the family. You and Pa just don't know about it."

Turning back to the girl sitting the horse he said, "Now listen careful: ride fast across the fields to the river. Cross upstream at the sandbar. The water's low, you should be able to get over without swimming him, but swim him, if you have to. Don't worry 'bout gettin' the saddle wet. Be careful coming up that steep west bank, but don't get off the horse. You have to move fast. Go to grandfather Decker's. Tell them Pa's been shot."

"Shot!" screamed sister Lea. "How do you know that Jakey?"

"Hush Lea," he said. Looking back up at Belietje he asked, "Did you hear me girl?"

"Yes!" she replied.

"Good! Tell Uncle John to come down the Kings road—warn the Cole family, then meet me at the Church ford. I'll follow Pennhorn road past the Van Aken's—pick up one or two of them along the way."

"Now Ride Girl!"

He stepped back and slapped Old Red across the rump as hard as he could. Belietie leaned forward in the saddle and quickly disappeared around the barn, with a clattering of rapid hoof beats.

As the horse and rider galloped across the hay field, the chilly night air felt cold on her skin, and Belietje felt something sticky on the saddle beneath her. As she rode, she reached out to give Old Red a pat on his neck. Again she felt the strange stickiness. Suddenly she realized. It was blood... her Papa's blood!

Warm tears welled up instantly in her blue eyes. Just as quick she leaned out over the horse's neck and began to beat Old Red across his rump with the loose ends of the leather reins, which she held tightly in her right hand.

Soon Old Red leaped headlong off the bank and into the river, but the water wasn't so low as Jakey had hoped. The horse had to swim. Belietje gasped as she was almost totally submerged in icy water. There was no time to squeal and no one to hear if she did. So she held on tight and set her teeth. She knew her father and brother were depending on her.

She emerged from the river still mounted, and still whipping Old Red, as he came stumbling and lunging up the west bank out into Grandfather Decker's big corn field.

Red was a strong horse and the girl was a light load. But, this had been a long, hard run. The big animal began to fail. Beleitje noticed his labored breathing as he came up the muddy riverbank. She knew he wanted and needed rest but she could not let off her expectations of him—not yet!

So, onward they sped, with thundering hooves tearing at the ground, soft earth flying up behind them, past cornstalks still shocked in the field, the girl crying silently and lashing the tired horse any time he slowed his advance, toward the dark form of the Decker barns, silhouetted now in the silver moonlight, on the low ridge, half a mile further west.

Chapter 21: The Shadow Of Death

Two days passed and the sun rose in a clear cold sky. That had been three hours ago. A hoary frost still clung to every branch, stalk, and blade of grass in the valley. The land shimmered in a crystalline splendor, which normally would have brought a smile to the face of young Belietje Davids, but not today. Today they were going to bury Pa.

The family walked beside the ox cart carrying Solomon Davids, Jr, from his father-in-law's house, slowly toward the burying grounds at the Dutch Reformed Church, near Machackemack Ford. Ironically they were traveling down the Kings Road,[14] the same trail Solomon had ridden behind his father on the big grey gelding, that rainy day in 1719. The day long ago, when he had first glimpsed his future bride, from behind her mother's skirt.

Today, thirty-five year old Lea (Decker) Davids walked silently at the right side of the cart, dressed in black. Her sixteen-year-old son Jacobus walked ahead, beside the lumbering red oxen. The ox team plodded steadily along, responding to an occasional prod, delivered gently by the boy with a hickory stick.

On the left side of the ox-cart strode eighteen-year-old daughter Lea, carrying her one-year-old brother Petrus. Following her, in order of their births, were the other Davids children: Belietje, Daniel, Joel, Jonas, Catherine, and finally three-year-old Elizabeth, skipped along, trying to keep up.

From time to time Elizabeth glanced back at her uncle Jorris. Elizabeth thought her uncle looked mad today. He was at the head of a large crowd of friends and family escorting her

---

[14] I know others refer to this as the Old Mine Road but in the records of the Minisink Precinct which were written at the time, the locally elected commissioners of the Kings by-ways, called it then "the Kings Road" and sometimes marked on the nearby trees (K.R.) to designate it as such.

father to his final resting place. Now that she thought about it, all the men following looked mad and all the women looked sad.

She hoped she hadn't done anything wrong. She really didn't understand this funeral business everyone kept talking about. She knew she was supposed to be mad or sad, she just wasn't exactly sure why.

Most of the crowd following behind the cart were neighbors, family, or friends. They had names like Westfall, Cole, Ennis, Van Aken, Quick, Swartwood and Westbrook. Many considered themselves New Jersey people, others were New Yorkers. But today they were all mourners.

As the procession turned off the road at the burying grounds, Reverend Fryenmoet trudged down the path from the church. Following him were many other mourners who had arrived from the south or from the east side of the Machackemack River down Pennhorn road past the Davids home and mill. New names were added to the large crowd now gathering, names like: Kortreght, Kuykendal, Middagh, Van Etten, Cuddebeck, Brinck, Chambers, Dewitt, Dingenman.

As the mourners positioned themselves around the bury hole, six of the men lowered the wooden casket into the ground. Most eyes were directed toward the earth. But a few people looked up to scan the crowd, catch the gaze of another, nod in recognition, and then look down again.

Reverend Fryenmoet stepped forward opening his Bible. He paused, listening. The crowd made a last minute shuffle into place.

"The Lord is my shepherd, I shall not want…" he began to read. The service was not long. In only a few minutes the reverend began to draw toward its close.

Belietje heard the words: "ashes to ashes and dust to dust..".

To escape being overcome by her grief, she stole a look out over the fields toward home. She noticed the frost and ice had melted and then she heard a pair of cardinals singing to one another. Shockingly she realized it was going to be a beautiful day.

The funeral ended. Neighbors and friends lingered with condolences, and offers of help. Soon Lea and her children were in the ox-cart with Jacobus driving the big team toward home. From the back of the cart Belietje noticed uncle Jorris, had stayed behind. He stood with a group of men under a large Oak, across the road from the church. He was speaking rapidly about something and the men were listening.

Belietje noticed Reverend Fryenmoet watching, from the church doorway, his arms folded across his chest. Uncle Jorris looked angry and the Reverend was chewing his lower lip as he sometimes did on Sundays, when he had temporarily lost his place during a sermon.

⁂

The evening chores waited when the Davids Family got home. The children went directly to the work. Soon they were gathering eggs, forking hay, hauling water, or spinning wool. Even little Elizabeth swept the hearth with her mother's broom. Only Lea herself seemed frozen in her grief. She sat at the table staring into the fire her eldest daughter and namesake had kindled.

Though Ma seemed dulled to the children, hundreds of thoughts were actually spinning around in her head. Most were memories of a life spent with the man now in the grave. But other thoughts were worries about the ten children they had conceived together: nine now drawing breath and one, which she carried within her.

⁂

Next morning, Jacobus awoke to the crack of an ax, the unmistakable sound of splitting wood, and the thump of a severed chunk hitting the ground. He and his brothers Daniel, Joel, and Jonas had slept in the barn, making room in the small stone house for uncle Jorris and aunt Debra, who had decided to sleep over. It was just now first light. The younger boys except for Daniel were snug, asleep, curled up in the yellow wheat-straw. Jacobus climbed down the ladder, slipped out the barn door and found Daniel at the woodpile.

"Little early this morning for all this noise isn't it?" he asked his brother.

Daniel was facing away, but he had heard the hinges as the door opened. He was in mid swing, when the words were spoken. The ax cracked again, another chunk split cleanly, falling to the ground. Then Daniel turned to face his brother:

"Couldn't sleep no more. Besides they're already a-stir in the house. Uncle Jorris left early on foot. Someone already has a fire going."

Jacobus glanced toward the stone house. Sure enough, white smoke shot up from the chimney, rising fast toward a crisp clear sky. "Smoke always rises straight as an arrow on cold mornings," he thought, "and wood splits clean and easy."

Daniel was a big boy, strong for his age. He normally helped Pa with the heavy work in the mill. But splitting wood on cold mornings had always been a special pleasure for him.

"Uncle Jorris is going to find out who did this, isn't he?" he asked.

"Well he's sure going to try Daniel. But, nobody seems to be talking much. I took him, right after, to the spot where we found Pa on the trail. We could tell from the tracks where Old Red took off, when the shot was fired. Pa was able to stay in the saddle only a short distance."

Jacobus stopped for a moment to clear the lump forming in his throat. Then he went on.

"From where Red lit out a-runnin, uncle Jorris and old Jake soon found the place in the woods where the killer stood. It looked like he had been waiting for a while. The forest duff was all mashed, like where deer have bedded down. Jake says it was sure a white man, but there weren't much sign left. Whoever he was, he weren't mounted and he went back up the trail, east toward the mountains. Hard to tell where he ended up. He may have had a horse hid somewhere higher up, or maybe he lives nearby."

Jacobus bent over, picked up a couple pieces of split wood and carried them a few paces to place them on the wood stack.

"Uncle Jorris says only one thing's for sure. It didn't have nothing to do with them hogs that old man Kittle was arguing with Mr. Westbrook about. Did you see them two at the funeral."

"Yeah I did," said Daniel.

"Well they both always liked Pa, about as much as they hated each other. Now their acting like brothers and threatening personally to burn any man who done this."

"Jakey, don't you think it had to do with the border?"

"Yeah. Maybe even—it was someone out of the valley. I know people around here get riled up against each other, but I'd hate to think one of our neighbors done it."

"Do you think, we might never know who done it."

"Maybe. But my guess is someone, sooner or later, will say something. Uncle Jorris says killers usually have to brag to someone. You know how most people talk. We'll find out!"

"What if it's someone just bragging he done it to look big?"

"Don't matter to me. The way I feel someone has to pay. If they done it and I find out, or if they brag they done it, or if I even think they might have done it. That's just the way I feel. So does uncle Jorris. Sooner or later someone is going to have to pay."

Jacobus stormed off toward the mill rubbing his eyes as he trudged up the hill.

Daniel drew another long cold breath into his lungs, reaching down to place another log on the chopping block. The cold day seemed to match his mood. He was happy to have a large pile of wood needing to be split.

Chapter 22: Solomon the Third

Christmas came and went. Winter was harsh. Snow drifted four and five foot deep throughout the valley.

There was adequate hay and fodder on the Davids farm, and in the barn. But, the little kill beside the mill froze solid. Jakey and Daniel were forced daily to cut ice from the mill- pond, so the livestock could reach enough water. In early February the pond itself froze to its depth. The boys then had no choice, but to drive the stock across their fields to the Machackemack River, and cut more holes in that ice so their animals could drink.

In late February, the days began to get longer, the sun warmed, the ice-melt began to flow across the surface. The little stream had running water again, though it flowed now over the top of a winter's ice formation. It took over a week of warm weather, before all the ice melted and they saw the familiar rocky bottom, of the little kill.

Early March was cold and rainy. With the ground still frozen beneath, snowmelt and rain caused the river to flood. Then followed a week of slush and mud. Finally, the valley had begun to dry out. April would soon be here. The river had returned to its banks. On high ground near the house and mill the earth solidified. Once more the family heard the clomp of heavy hooves on solid, unfrozen ground.

Not only the grass but the trees too, began to green, with that early soft green of catkins and new leaves before they have fully formed and darkened. Spring had come at last, and it brought with it a new energy. Life seemed to be everywhere.

One afternoon, late in March, the cry of a new baby called out from the Davids' farmstead to greet the honking of a thousand black and white geese just landing in the fields between him and the river.

A month later, Lea Davids had her new son in the Machackemack Church to participate in another familiar christening ceremony. She had decided to name her tenth child after his father and grandfather. The family arrived early as did most of the congregation, but the services began with uncle Jorris coming in the doorway and removing his hat at the very last moment.

Jorris had made the eight-mile ride from Kendiamong this morning. During the ride he had been reminiscing about his life, which until recently had been enter-twined with the life of his brother Solomon. As boys they had hunted and fished with their Munsi friends. But on many days they had roamed the Minisink's woods and streams together, just the two, never seeing another human.

Those had been good times, Jorris recalled. Neither had then owned a musket. But, they had both been as accomplished with bow and arrow as the Munsi youths. Venison and small game of all kind found its way to the Davids family table. Fur and skins were traded for fishhooks, knives and tomahawks.

In those times wolves howled nightly in the valley. Elk and bear were often about in early morning. Sign of lynx and panther were frequent. Sometimes the big cats were seen for a fleeting moment, crossing a trail, or the edge of some pasture, at daybreak or dusk.

One night, Jorris and Solomon had been picking and feeling their way along a nighttime trail in the Shawagunks. They were inching along trying hard not to stumble in the dark. Suddenly a deafening scream pierced the stillness. Momentarily, both boys were riveted to the trail, frozen in their fear.

"What the devil was that?" whispered Solomon.

Frantically they floundered about, retrieving arrows from quivers, and nocking them into bowstrings. But then they paused. In the inky blackness, they could see nothing at which to aim.

The scream came a second time, louder than the first. Whatever was near them, in the darkness, sounded plenty dangerous. Jorris could hear the sound of Solomon's steady breath over his shoulder. It steadied him. Back to back, they stood, waiting, listening. Together they strained to sense, from where the danger might leap upon them. Nothing stirred. Moments passed like hours.

Finally there was a rustle of the leaves above, then the sudden swish of branches springing down—then up again. The big cat was moving off leaping from limb to limb through the treetops.

Gradually that sound faded away. The brothers were left standing in the darkness listening once again to the innocent sounds of peepers and crickets. A soft, gentle, breeze and their own breathing seemed the only things now stirring along the ridgeline.

The memory of that night was almost thirty years old, yet, Jorris could feel the hair stiffen on the back of his neck, now, at the thought of standing with his brother waiting for the cat to decide. Together, that night, they had appeared too strong for the big cat.

Perhaps, if Jorris had been riding alongside his brother on that fateful night last October, the assassin might also have reconsidered, slinking off in the darkness. But Jorris had not been riding with Solomon. The killer had struck. That regret taunted him now, daily. Today Jorris was here in the church, but his thoughts kept wondering…

Belietje stood with her family near the front of the small church sanctuary. Machackemack church like the church near Minisink Island was built of stone. Today the window shudders and wooden doors were closed. Candles provided only a dim, dancing light, casting vague shadows on the cold walls.

"Ma is having a good day today," thought Belietje.

Lea Davids had been in a terrible state of melancholy since her husband's murder. Most days she simply sat inside her house—In the dark—unless someone else lit a candle or built up the fire. The children kept up the chores, and never let the fire grow cold. The boys did a solid job of it, keeping the animals alive over winter. But, soon, the planting would need to begin, and then the milling business would resume. Grandfather Decker and Ma's brothers would come to help, but the family needed Ma back to herself. But, Lea (Decker) Davids seemed still far away, lost most days in her own private misery.

The majority of the people in the valley had been shocked by Solomon's murder, but Belietje knew others had not been surprised. Some even said her pa had been asking for trouble and got what he deserved. Those sentiments infuriated her, but the comments were never made in her presence or the family's.

Tuesday a week ago, Uncle Jorris had confronted Joshua Miller about just such a rumored remark. Her brother Daniel and Jorris had found Joshua at the blacksmiths, having a horse shod. Belietje did not know the details, but she knew a violent argument had occurred. It ended abruptly, when uncle Jorris grabbed a curing wooden axe handle and struck Joshua in the forehead. The blow had opened a large cut in Millers head.

According to Daniel, the impact knocked Joshua to his knees and took the starch right out of him. Daniel said as he and Uncle Jorris rode away, the blacksmith had dragged Joshua and propped him up against the water trough. The smith was busy with a rag blotting at the prodigious bleeding from Millers head. But Danniel said the blood was still dripping from Millers chin last he saw.

Old Jake, found out later, that Miller was able to mount his horse, with some assistance, and ride home by himself. Jake said the rest of the community was buzzing about the incident. But the Miller family had become unusually silent.

"We ask a special blessing upon Lea Davids, her late husband Solomon and their new son Solomon the third; bless also their witnesses, Jacobus Swartwood and Anetje Westbrook." Began the Reverend's prayer.

The Cole's baby suddenly began to cry. It startled Belietje, and brought her momentarily back to the present. But then her thoughts wondered.

"Why couldn't people understand?" Belietje asked herself: "Pa was just trying to keep the peace and some hot head killed him for it. Now the merciless coward is walking around somewhere, acting like nothing has happened. I could kill him myself, if I just knew who to kill."

She thought all this, without pause to consider where she was standing. But Belietje did not know who to blame and neither it seemed did anyone else.

"We ask a special blessing today upon Johannes Cole, his wife Nelli Van Aken and their new son Willem; bless also their witnesses, Willem Cole and Tjaetje Cole". (Multiple, Minisink Valley Reformed Dutch Church Records, 1915)

A stiff cold breeze blew through the valley this morning, and the timbers of the church roof answered with what Belietje thought was a mournful sound. She listened to the wood joints creak for a moment, accompanied by the reverends monotone. She thought it matched her mood almost exactly.

"We ask a special blessing upon Thomas Schoonhoven and his wife Myra Wesfael and their new son David bless also their witnesses David Cole and Tjetje Cole. (Multiple, Minisink Valley Reformed Dutch Church Records, 1915)

"It is odd," Belietje thought, "here we have Westbrooks and Swartwoods, Westfalls and Coles all, together, in the same Church, asking for God's blessings on these three baby boys. Wouldn't it be a special blessing for them all, if God could command the King and his Royal Governors, to settle the border dispute between New Jersey and New York—before anyone else gets killed."

"This concludes our services for this the 5th day of April in the year of our lord Seventeen hundred and fifty two. May God's blessings be upon you all. Amen." Fryenmoet concluded.

 "Amen," responded the congregation.

"God save King George," said Fryenmoet.

"God save the King," responded the crowd.

Chapter 23: Peter's Point

Jorris hugged his sister-in-law Lea, as she held in her arms the newly christened baby Solomon. He left the church without saying anything to anyone. Outside he mounted his roan horse. He looked back to nod at Belietje as she emerged through the doorway. Then he turned his horse north.

Belietje watched him urge the roan into a cantor up the King's Road. Then he reined his mount left, along a pathway, heading toward the Delaware River bottoms. She knew there were only a few homesteads off in that direction. Soon the flatlands would peter out and the mountains would come down to meet the river. She wondered where he might be going.

Jorris rode steadily along, with sadness settling once more upon him. This should have been a joyful day. But he did not feel joy.

Jorris had never liked 'jawing' with people. As a boy he had more in common with the Munsi than the white folks of the valley. In fact, most people had been quite surprised, when he had courted and married Debra Scoonhoven, (Multiple, Minisink Valley Reformed Dutch Church Records, 1915) taking up a small homestead at Kendiamong.

Even Solomon Jr. had wondered if Jorris could give up his hunting long enough to work a plantation. Jorris admitted to himself, at the time, he had suffered plenty of self-doubt. In the beginning it had been a struggle. But he had become a good husband, father and farmer.

Jorris took the time to work his fields, when they needed tending. He did not have the largest farmstead, and since he was still one of the best woodsmen in the valley, the family had never been hungry, even in the worst winters.

But Jorris had never developed the art of conversation. Now, he needed to know everything his neighbors might know, about his brother's killer. More than that, he was interested even in what they might think, or suspect.

So, over the months, he had acquired a habit of showing up on farmsteads, at inconvenient times. He would appear suddenly from out of the brush, seldom using the trails or normal byways. He did not have to say much. His quiet, somber manner made people very uncomfortable. Soon their tongues were wagging away to fill up the silence.

Over these past months, Jorris had discovered much about the feuds and fears between families and neighbors: Who refused to pay damages when their hogs had eaten the neighbors garden; who might have gathered their neighbors pigs from the woods notching their ears with his own markings; which mans sons were welcome to call on this families daughters and which ones might just as well stay to home; who couldn't be trusted around women folk from any mans family; who was honest as the day was long, and who would steel wood from his own deer uncles dwindling woodstack; stories of strange voices, heard on the Kings Road, when the moon was dark; who had seen, with his own eyes, Indians on the trail to Coshecton, but they were too far off to be counted; who had witnessed savages in canoes, south of Minisink Island just as they were disappearing into a fog bank; stories of strange footprints found along nearby bogs or stream banks; who was losing chickens, hogs, or sheep, or even horses; whose favorite dog had suddenly stopped barking night before last and hadn't been seen since.

Yes, Jorris had learned all sorts of things about happenings in the valley, but he did not feel closer to finding Solomon's' killer. He was beginning to fear that maybe he never would. It troubled him.

Today, Jorris rode past three farms, without slowing the pace of the roan. Rounding a bend in the trail he saw Peter Decker ahead, resting a team of oxen. Peter and his plodding beasts had just finished a pass, with the plow. They were pausing momentarily at the end of their field, before beginning the task of turning up the next small ridge of river-bottom dirt.

When Peter saw Jorris approaching he pulled his plow from the furrow and laid it over upon the ground. As he rose from the effort he was shocked. Jorris galloped by with only a tip of his hat.

It was unheard of, for people to leave a citizen standing by the trail, without a word. Peter had not seen a human outside his own family, for over a week. He was disappointed and puzzled.

It was rude behavior for a man to pass by a citizen, without stopping to jaw a bit about the happenings of the valley. He watched the horse and rider gallop away and wondered: "Where the devil does he think he's going?"

Beyond Decker's farm the trail narrowed, hugging the river, with the mountains coming down almost to the water. Here, a faint game track turned northeastward, up the slope. Jorris slowed his horse to a walk, turned his mount and urged the animal to begin the long climb.

The trail soon followed a switchback pattern, folding back upon itself, as it ascended the steep incline. Deer and elk hooves, kept this track worn into the mountainside as the animals took the path of least resistance, hugging the slope, first one way and then the other, to avoid climbing straight up. Twice the path emerged from cover of the trees, to pass a rocky outcrop. Here, only a few scraggly shrubs grew in the thin soil.

At the second overlook Jorris stopped to rest his horse. Below him, he could see the sparkling surface of the Fishkill, which most people now called the Delaware. He knew the river well. This stretch, with its submerged boulders and foaming spray, contained many dangers, when the water ran high.

Jorris dismounted now, stepping cautiously out on the rocks, toward the edge, to get a better view.

"You can see a lot from here!" he thought.

He noticed every riffle and every slick deep hole in the river showing clearly from above. Westward beyond the Delaware, he looked out over the mountains of Pennsylvania.

"A week of travel over there would bring me to the Susquehanna. I wonder if Otter is well?"

Remounting, Jorris looked up the slope. He thought for a moment he could see blue sky, above the ridge.

"We must be getting close to the top," he thought.

But the top was always farther away than it seemed on a climb. It took another half hour of scrambling to reach the ridge. Then he turned the horse right, along a narrow path heading off to the southward. The sharp scream of a brightly colored Jay announced Jorris's arrival on top. Then promptly the bird flew off sideways through the clear sky above the treetops toward a tall hickory on the next ridge to the northeast.

In a few minutes, a little nuthatch flitted ahead from tree to tree, showing him the way. Jorris and his big roan broke out of the tall pines finally, onto the rocky point of a headland. There was a short patch of grass between the trees and the ledge of a south-facing precipice.

Jorris dismounted, and tethered his horse to a scraggly Pine. As he did, he watched the rocks nearby. A snake just might be lying in the warmth of this afternoon's sun. He smiled.

Jorris patted his horses' neck, running his hands along its jaw, he gripped his mount by the chin and placed the Roan's muzzle against his own cheek in an affectionate little hug. The horse sniffed the air, curled his upper lip, turned his head to one side, to get a better look, and stared back with a huge, liquid-brown, eye.

"You've had a hard ride old friend," said Jorris. "It's time for a rest."

The big animal gave a wet snort shaking his head and covered Jorris suddenly with a splattering of wet horse slobber. Stepping back, Jorris smiled again and wiped his face on his shirtsleeve. Then he began to loosen the saddle girth strap.

Quickly the saddle and his other duffel were on the ground and the horse was hobbled. The big animal snorted again, shuddered to shed a few flies, flicked his tail with a snap and began to graze on the thin mountain grass.

The day had warmed and it was pleasant in spite of a steady wind, which always seemed to buffet everything up this high.

Jorris wasn't sure why he had been drawn here, but he was glad he had come. As youngsters he and Solomon had visited the bluff often. It was a long way from Kendiamong. But in summer they had sometimes come here, to stay overnight, enjoying the cool mountain breeze. Jorris thought this might be just the place to ponder his problems.

He was not ready to forgive or forget. He wanted his pound of flesh. But so far, he simply did not know where to direct his anger.

He could not retaliate against someone on the other side, because it was not clear which was the other side. Most likely it was a Yorker. But Solomon had provoked denunciations from New Jersey families too. Belligerent threats had been rumored against him from both sides.

Most of the local elders, regardless of their stand in the conflict, had been vocally supportive of Solomon. He personally had enjoyed many friends among the established families of the valley. Many people had trusted him, exactly because he had not played favorites to either side in the dispute.

Recently, however, the growing families and a steady flow of new settlers had exacerbated the need for more land. Land was the only path available to most people for any kind of financial security. What had once been merely an annoyance between neighbors now had become a struggle for dominance.

Someone had interpreted the contentious rhetoric, spouted by the hotheads of the valley, as a call to war. Regrettably that had resulted in the killing of a good man.

People had now suspended their petty bickering, long enough to contemplate what might happen next. Who else might get killed? Did they really want a war with their neighbors?

Jorris pondered these issues himself, as he picked his way carefully over the jagged rocks, jutting up from the thin soil, to the south rim of Peters' point. People had begun calling the bluff that name, because it overlooked Peter Decker's farm. As Jorris approached the edge of the cliff now, he saw Peter and his team, far below, making another slow plodding pass across his field, turning up one more thin ribbon of shiny black soil.

What people call the Minisink Valley is actually parts of two separate valleys. The Delaware River springs from headwaters on the western slopes of the Catskill Mountains. It flows around and through those highlands, in a wide westward arc of hundreds of miles, before it comes back to approach the Minsink flowing in a southeasterly direction.

The Machackemack River[15] has its headwaters on the southern slopes of the same Catskill Mountains. But this river follows a shorter sweep westward, flowing then back to the east, where it meets the Shawagunk Mountains and turns a final time to enter the Minisink valley flowing southwesterly.

Both rivers are flanked by highlands, which parallel their course, hundreds and sometimes thousands of feet above their waters. At places along the journey the mountains come down sharply to the water's edge. At other locations there are flat bottomlands stretching out on one or both sides of the rivers.

Sometimes these flatlands between the river and the sharp slopes of the mountains can be as much as few miles wide. These lowlands have black fertile soils growing luxurious healthy plants. The Minisink valley was such a place. Fields had been cleared here for farming generations before white men ever came.

Facing south, the left slope of the Delaware highlands and the right slope of the Machackemack highlands come together to form this precipice called Peters Point about a mile north of

---

[15] The Machackemack branch would later be named the Neversink River.

where the waters from the two rivers converge. On a clear day the rim of the cliff provides a one thousand foot elevated vista of 280 degrees up, across, and down the two valleys. Only the most northerly directions are blocked from view by the trees.

Today there was a huge expanse of blue sky, interrupted only by a few small, sailing, white clouds. Below, lie newly greened fields and woodlands, brilliantly displayed, in the sunshine. It was one of those days, when you can see for a long, long, way.

Southward Jorris could see the waters of the Delaware make a wide bend, shifting the big rivers direction to the southwest. At the far end of that bend he could just make out the mouth of the Machackemack, as it opened into the Delaware, at a narrow spit of sand called Carpenters point.

Here, at Carpenters Point, different raindrops, which might have fallen to earth only a few feet apart on a ridge in the Catskill Mountains, finally were united after flowing hundreds of miles in different directions. From here, they would stream together, through the remaining forty miles of the Minisink Valley. Then flowing through the mountains at the Water Gap, they would roll on hundreds more miles, passed the small but growing, inland port city of Philadelphia[16], and finally blend with the briny waters of the Delaware Bay and Atlantic Ocean.

Jorris loved the immediate view, which lay before him. It provided him an entirely different perspective on the world, than he ever saw from the valleys' floor. From up here, everything below seemed to move slowly. Even sound was delayed, as it reverberated across the greater distances. The scene seemed always to have a tranquil affect upon him, and today was no different.

Looking downriver, beyond the point, Jorris squinted, trying to focus his eyes. He thought today he might be able to see

---

[16] A small, but growing town of roughly twenty thousand people at this time.

the nine miles, all the way to Kendiamong but he was not sure. Off to the left a few degrees, he could see clearly the Kittatinny Ridge stretching far away to the southwest. He knew that on the eastern slopes of those mountains lay the valley of the Pualinskill and the log jail of the recently formed Sussex county New Jersey.

Further to the left and much closer, Jorris could see the open slash in the woodlands, where the Machackemack River split its valley floor into east and west halves. Immediately to the southwest of his position on the bluff and this side of that river, was an opening in the trees, where Jorris knew the Church and burying grounds were built. Nearer, on the same line, he could see a thin ribbon of smoke rising up out of the trees. He knew that smoke was from the fireplace of Willem Cole.

From Cole's place his eyes scanned northward, until he spotted the open fields of the John Decker Farm. These were some of the oldest and largest fields in this part of the valley. The Decker barns were visible from here and even the stone chimney of the house could be seen through the treetops, its white wood-smoke rising toward the heavens.

Looking on across the valley a mile or two more, to the northeast, on the far side of the river, where the slopes of the Shawagunk Mountains began to rise up, he saw another column of white wood-smoke. He knew this smoke was from the mill and farm of his late brother Solomon. Jorris's own nieces had probably kindled that fire to cook up a pot of beans and salt pork, or some other fixings for their supper.

He sniffed the air. No hint of wood smoke. No pork. Just Pine needles. Horse sweat. A redolence of spring plowing.

The thought of Solomon's family brought back his sorrow. It rankled Jorris that he had not been there to help his brother at his time of greatest need. It plagued him more that he had since been unable to avenge his brother's murder. Solomon had been a good brother, husband and father. He deserved better.

Jorris had been a dangerous man in the early months after his brother's murder. He had been anxious to punish someone—anyone!

He shuddered now to think of what he might have done—of the mistakes he might have made. More than once he had sighted down the barrel of his musket at the chest or back of some neighbor only to awaken from his dream just before or after he pulled the trigger.

Twice he had not awakened because it had not been in a dream. Both these times he had simply reconsidered at the last moment, reluctantly removing his finger from the trigger, disappearing back into the forest, leaving the suspected neighbor rubbing their eyes wondering if maybe they had imagined the whole frightening experience.

Killing a man was not easy for Jorris. It required, for him, a certainty, which had been hard to find.

Uncommonly the killer had proved not to be a fool or a braggart. Perhaps only the assassin himself knew who he was.

"If he keeps his mouth shut," Jorris thought, "maybe, I never will find him out."

He was overcome with the frustration and rage, which had built up within him for months. His legs felt suddenly weak. He lowered himself down to sit on a rock. He placed his face in his hands and leaned forward. He shivered. Then he yielded to the agony of his grief. His broad shoulders heaved as he sobbed. His hat fell to the ground.

─────── ✢ ───────

Jorris did not cry long. When he finished he dried his tears on his shirtsleeve and was astonished to find how relieve he felt. A great weight, it seemed, had been lifted from him. Yet he knew nothing had actually changed.

Picking up his hat and pulling it down on his head Jorris peered out across the valley searching for landmarks to indicate the other farmsteads he knew were there. As he was looking for the Van Aken and Westfall farms, he saw instead a shadow passing across the woodlands and fields. Glancing up to the sky, he observed a small cloud sailing between the sun and the earth, producing the shadow, which moved over the landscape. Just below and beyond the cloud, a hawk circled in the high winds. He could see the bird was casting its own tiny shadow, which also circled upon the countryside displayed below.

He wondered what might be seen from the bird's perspective: "From there, I might be able to see beyond the Kittatinny. Yes, I think I could. And from where the cloud is, I would likely be able to see over the Shawagunks too.

He knew he could not continue his search for vengeance as he had been doing. "I need to pace myself." He thought: "It might take years."

"Maybe time will provide me a new perspective and I'll find out what I need to know. Until then, I must wait, watch and listen. I won't forget. When the time comes, I'll know."

Jorris rose from the rock and picked his way back to where his horse was tethered. Quickly he rolled out his bedroll. The sun was still high. It would take time to get his camp set and gather a night's firewood. He glanced off to the northeast and saw again the white wood-smoke from the Davids' Mill, there, across the valley. This time he smiled at his thoughts about his brother. He spoke aloud to his brother's spirit.

"You always liked it up here didn't you Sol. Well, tonight we'll sleep up here, together again, just the two of us, like in the old days. Maybe you can send me a sign or somthin."

Jorris smiled once more, turned and sauntered off, along the ridge, his head down, searching the ground for pine knots.

Chapter 24: War

*E*arly July, 1754, was hot and dry. Wheat harvest was over and yellow stacks of straw dotted the fields like giant beehives. Jakey was in the mill helping Daniel grind flour for Mr. Ennis, when he heard the old man call out:

"Hey boys, shut her down fer a minute and come out here. You got company."

When the boys stepped out of the mill, Mr. Ennis and old Jake Kuckendal stood at the water trough. Jake's big bay horse was shiny-slick with dripping sweat and the gelding was busy slurping up all the mossy, green water from the wooden trough, like he hadn't seen a drink in a long while.

"Good morning Jake," said Daniel.

"Mornin boys" was the reply from the old trader, "But I'm not sure how good it is. I got bad news. I was down river to Easton day before yesterday. Looks like there's war tween' us and the French. And looks like they've already joined up most of the Indians to fight fer' them."

"Was they Indian trouble in Easton?" Mr. Ennis asked.

"No! Not in Easton, not yet anyway."

"The Virginians had trouble way out in the western parts of their own country. A place called Great Meadow. Their governor sent a hundred Red-coats, and about three times that many Virginia militia, to protect some traders building a post at the Forks of the Ohio. Somehow the army got into a little scrap with some Frenchy officer named Jumonville and he got hisself killed. That was in late May. Next thing they knowed, a month later, there's French Regulars and Indians swarming in from all over. So our boys took off fer home."

Old Jake rose up in the saddle, stretching his neck and arching his back with a sigh. He'd been riding hard and he was just about done in.

"It's hard country out there by the Forks," he said. "They had to make a stand at this place called Great Meadow. Some twenty-one-year-old colonel, named Washington, was in command. There was a big battle and the Virginians had a little picketed fort they had thrown up kinda fast, but the trees was too close around it. You know them cowardly French; they just hid out behind those trees, picking off Red-coats and Colonials one at a time."

"The king's soldiers threw a couple good charges at them. But the French and Indians just pulled back and then came up to the tree line again, when the Red-coats retreated back into the fort. To make matters worse it come a toad strangling rain and wet all the gunpowder.

The Soldiers and Virginians were outnumbered four to one. The French commander sent word in that he couldn't protect anyone from being scalped, or worse, unless they all surrendered at once. They didn't have much choice—so they did."

The old trader leaned forward, to stroke and pat his horse's neck. He wiped the horse-sweat from his hands onto his breeches.

"The French let 'em all march fer' home the next day, with their flags a-flying. But the wretched Indians, flanked 'em fer' a whole day more, ransacking their baggage at will and taking whatever they wanted. I heard the story from a man that was there. He said they were all lucky, to get home with their hair still on their heads. He was some shook up. Said he had never seen so many Indians or Frenchmen either."

Daniel and Jakey looked at each other, but said nothing.

"Well what's going to happen here?" asked Mr. Ennis.

"I don't know for sure, maybe nothing—but I doubt we're that lucky. If there is a war with the French we better be gettin' ourselves ready. To the west and northwest there ain't nothing but hills and trees 'tween us and them. 'Specially if they get any of the western Iroquois tribes to join their fight."

Jake pulled the horse's head away from the trough and look thoughtfully across the river to the west. He hesitated and then let the horse return to the water.

"They say some of the Shawnee were with the French, but no-one saw any of the Delaware Indians or Iroquois. Maybe they ain't decided yet. We have to keep scouts out and start thinking about how best to fort up if we need to. Some folks from Upper Smithfield[17] are already thinkin' about movin' back to this side of the Fishkill. They're really exposed over there if the Shawnee have struck the war post."

"The Virginians are raisin' an army. I'm sure New Jersey and New York will too. Who knows about the Quakers. But we'll be on our own till they get organized and go whip them Frogs[18], and their Indians."

"Your uncle Jorris is spreading the news on the other side of the Machackemack. We've already sent out a few scouts. We'll meet at the church Sunday to decide what else needs to be done. I better get on along, up toward Peenpack. We don't want anyone asleep if them devils come here."

With the reins, he once again jerked his horse's head away from the water and this time he mounted. He looked back down at Jakey and Daniel.

"Boys, don't let the children or women stray. Keep your muskets and pistols primed, and near. Keep your animals up close at night."

The old trader looked thoughtfully to the eastward, up the slope of the nearby mountain. He nodded that way:

"We'll have someone scouting that ridge but keep a close eye on it. Your danger here is from that direction. If they come at

---

[17] The uppermost, sparsely populated, township of Northampton County Pennsylvania, which lie directly across the Delaware River opposite the Minisink Valley

[18] This was a derogatory slang term used by Englishmen and others for Frenchmen.

us from any other way there are plenty of farms they will hit first and you will hear the fight or see the smoke. But if they get to the east of us and come back from there you may be the first place hit. That's your most danger.

"You won't have much time if they come but try to get off some shots and fire something up to warn your neighbors. Then get inside the house, or away, as fast as you can. It's unlikely they will come that way but you got to be ready."

With that said the old trader turned his horse north and nudged him into a slow gallop up Pennhorn road.

Mr. Ennis and the boys watched him go. Jakey turned to Daniel.

"You get the flour finished for Mr. Ennis. I'll go get the muskets and tell Ma and the girls." That said he trotted off toward the house.

Daniel and Mr. Ennis started back toward the mill. As they walked toward the doorway their eyes were drawn up slope across the little pasture, which terminated at a rail fence. That grass and the little rail fence was all that separated them from the trees and the sharp slope of the mountain. Beyond the fence, were thousands of acres of forests and highlands, coves, ridges, and peaks, which could conceal a whole army if one wished to hide there.

Chapter 25: Braddock's Defeat

$\mathcal{A}$ year passed. July was starting off, hot as usual. The locusts had returned this summer. They were already singing loudly from woodlands and fields. It had become a ringing in your ear, which you thought might never stop.

The Davids family was late to church. They arrived to find the place a-buzz with people.

Old Jake Kuckendal was in the pulpit, which was a strange sight because old Jake had never stood there before. He cleared his throat to speak. Everyone hushed. The old trader spoke clearly, his voice booming through the stillness of the crowd gathered in the stone sanctuary. His words echoed a bit off the walls.

"I got more bad news" He began. "You all know about General Braddock, and his two thousand red-coats sent by King George to punish the French for what they done last summer at Great Meadows. That army marched out through Virginia in mid-June heading to the Forks Of the Ohio. They had along with 'em another thousand or so Colonials. It was a big army."

He paused, to clear his throat and sigh. Jake looked like a feller whose favorite horse had just broken a leg and he was about to put him down for good.

"The news is they been badly beaten. The General hisself is dead. Most of his officers are dead. And the word is, over a thousand of his soldiers are dead too."

Old Jake paused and his words sank in deep. Then he continued.

"The survivors were chased almost a hundred miles. They say that same Colonel—named Washington—from Virginia, had to take charge again when the general was killed. Washington got the boys back in some order, but most of the serious wounded had to be left behind to the savages. The baggage train was overrun too and all the women camp followers was drug off or killed."

There was a quiet gasp from old Mrs. Cole and a few whispers in the back of the room.

When things quieted, Jake went on.

"The French have loosed their dogs on our frontier. The devils are raiding all over. Some of the Delaware, who were living out in the Ohio Country, were with 'em this time, along with the Shawnee and the Huron. Likely other tribes have been waiting to see how this fight would turn out. Now they may throw in with the French, and if they do, there will be hell to pay."

The old trapper glanced toward Fryenmoet and said: "Sorry Reverend. "Then he spoke again. "They say that Pennsylvania is building a string of forts up through the Blue Mountains, all the way to Shawnee, down in Lower Smithfield Township. But they ain't built yet. They ain't planning no more, up this way, on their side of the river.

New Jersey is supposed to be a-building us a string of forts up our side of the river, they say. But none of them ain't started yet either. North of us Jury Westfall is startin' to fortify his house, but 'tween there and Marbletown is a mighty big gap."

"Far as I know, New York won't be sending no help this way. They seem too worried about their northern and Mohawk frontiers. I'm a-feared they will forget us like usual. We cain't expect much help from that direction."

He paused again looking as if he didn't know what to say next.

"We'll keep scouts out but everyone's gonna have to do his part. There's a thousand ways the devils can get through or around us. They might come at us, from any direction, on any day. You all have to stay alert and sound the alarm so folks can get to safety. We need to be thinkin about building us a fort real soon. That's all I got to say. God help us."

Old Jake looked worried as he stepped away from the pulpit. Reverend Fryenmoet stepped forward with his bible:

"Let us pray…" said the reverend.

The religious service today was short. People soon came out the church-house door. Some went quickly for home. Some, including the Davids family, milled about wondering what else they might learn. Belietje stood near the door and watched her brothers standing in front of the church with several other men.

Some of the fellows were quiet and thoughtful. Others spoke in agitated, angry, or nervous, tones. The churchyard sounded like a cornfield where a new flock of geese had just landed, all giving their opinion on the safety or dangers of the feeding ground and all trying to be heard at the same time.

Nearby Belietje heard a man named Vandam speaking to a friend of his. He spoke loudly. Most people close heard what he had to say:

"I'm leaving the valley for Goshen as soon as I can get packed. You'd be wise to get your family and come with us. This ain't no place to be with children and womenfolk if there's goin to be a war with the Injins and French."

He didn't wait for his friend to answer or even consider. He just rushed off toward his family waiting down the road a-piece.

Mr. Cole heard his comment, and turned to Jacobus: "Easy enough fer him." he said nodding toward the man leaving. "He ain't got much to move. He just came here a couple years ago–would have starved the first winter if your grandpap Decker hadn't given him enough turnips and pumpkins to get his family through till spring."

Mr. Cole looked down at the ground to kick a little rock with the side of his boot-toe. He took a deep breath and said, "I guess everyone will have to make his own decisions. I ain't telling no man what to do with his family. Maybe we're fools to stay but I ain't leavin' just because of what might happen. Your Grandpap Davids always did say 'The Frogs and their

Huron Dogs ought to be shot on sight'. I guess he'll be getting his wish."

"Yeah, grandpap always hated the French."said Jakey. "And the French Indians. They burnt up his uncle Christoffelson and his family in their cabin up in Schenectady. They slaughtered almost a whole village that night. I guess that was reason enough fer Grandpap to hate 'em fer a lifetime. I recon he was right. Now it looks like we're gonna have to fight 'em all over again."

"Well it ain't just the French Indians with the Frenchies this time. It's the Shawnee and the Ohio Tribes and probably the Delaware too. If we don't start winning some of these fights they may turn the whole Iroquois Six Nations against us. If them boys start thinkin their backing the losing side they'll turn. I don't trust any of 'em, except, maybe, the Mohawk," said Mr. Cole.

"Yeah," said Jakey. "Well maybe that's why Albany, ain't sending us no help. They need to look strong up North, to keep the Iroquois on King George's side, or at least neutral, and out of the fight."

"Maybe. Course out here it don't matter much, whether you get killed by a Shawnee or an Iroquois, either way we'll be just as dead. Thank God the Jersey's ain't abandoned us—yet," said Cole.

"Do you believe the Munsi, in the Susquehanna Valley, will join with the French in this fight?" asked Jakey.

"Well, I know what your Pa would have thought. He always said they'd be back to reclaim their lands. He and your Uncle Jorris, and your grandpap Davids, and Old Jake: they all said the Pennsylvanians would pay for that Walking Treaty trick. They said it weren't right.

That's sure enough how the Munsi saw it and I'm guessing that's why we'll have to fight em now. So, I recon we might as well get ready. Everyone is gonna have to pick a side now—like it or not.

Chapter 26: The Fort

$\mathcal{F}$rom the day Jake Kuckendal brought news of the War, the Davids family watched their little pasture to the east, with a new understanding, and dread. After Braddock's Defeat at the battle of Monongahela[19] they watched it even closer. They were keenly aware of the danger, which might someday emerge from the forest, in that direction. But only squirrel, raccoon and the occasional deer strayed into the grassy clearing to keep company with the two cows and three sheep.

As the year advanced, color seemed to flow down the mountainside, like molasses on a cold December morning. In a few weeks the landscape eased from summer green to a myriad of yellow, orange and red. Maple and hickory, sumac and poison ivy, put on their brightest displays of the season, and then faded. The leaves fell away except for the stubborn oaks and beech trees which held on to a few of their own dry, brown relics. Soon those shriveled remaining leaves began pecking at their giant matriarchs, as if trying desperately to regain their attention. Energized by a steady winter breeze, they were the origin of that tap, tap, tapping sound, so familiar to every hunter and scout in the valley.

And then overnight came the snow, blanketing the countryside in a cold, undisturbed, whiteness. With this first snowfall everyone's apprehension waned.

War parties were less likely in winter. It was difficult to travel over mountains covered in ice. It was harder to live off the land this time of year and almost impossible to hide tracks in

---

[19] The significance of Braddock's Defeat, to folks of that time is difficult for Americans in our century to appreciate. It would help, I think, to compare it to the attack on Pearl Harbor for our parents or grandparents generation, or the attack of Nine-Eleven in our own time. But then, you might still have to multiply the shock effect, by whatever number you think appropriate, when you consider, that there were no oceans, separating their homes and children from the enemy.

new fallen snow. Attacks in winter were not unheard of, but they were rare.

This winter was cold with wonderfully lots of snow. But fortunately the mill pond did not freeze to its bottom this year. Life in the Minisink seemed almost normal by Christmas.

The deep snow was lovely and the Davids family celebrated for over a week at Grandfather Decker's. They took their meals inside the small stone house but slept in the barn loft with Aunts, Uncles and dozens of cousins.

Belietje liked sleepin' in the loft of granddad's big barn. The gentle lowing of the cattle in the stalls below, the seemingly endless crunching sounds of cows chewing and re-chewing, the sweet-sour smell of manure mixed with the distinct aroma of hay, straw, oats, corn, wheat, rye, and barley all blended into an olfactory feast, pleasing to her country-girl senses. It was cold but with all the animals and people crowded into the tight space it was always ten degrees warmer inside than out.

What the children called wolf dens were hollowed out spaces in the straw lined with quilts and blankets. Wolf packs made up of mothers and fathers, brothers sisters and a stray cousin or two which everyone referred to as stray pups, snuggled warmly together, yapping and howling well into the night. Belietje missed her Pa sorely but it was a relaxed fun time. War worries seemed temporarily on hold, at least for the children. Even Ma was caught once or twice smiling at some of the frolics.

Reverend Fryenmoet had agreed with his congregation that the church was a natural place to be fortified. Pine logs were piled now all around the little stone building. More were being snaked in daily over the snow.

"How's the fort coming?" asked Grandfather Decker holding up his cup from where he sat in his house, in his chair, beside a hickory fire. The fire leaped toward the flue in the huge stone fireplace.

Belietje watched and listened from where she leaned herself against a cold outside wall, with little Petrus asleep in her lap. There were at least two dozen family members crowded into the little house right now, relaxing after supper, and listening to the old folks. Uncle John stepped forward watching out not to step on anyone's leg or foot. Carefully he refilled granddads cup from the jug.

"It's goin' good Pa. There are two log corner houses built now, one on the northwest and the other on northeast. The church itself will make the southwest corner. The Southeast will be a regular block house, and we'll have it done in a few days.

The corner buildings are each separated by about a hundred and twenty feet. As soon as the ground thaws and dries up a bit, we'll dig the trenches and start standing the poles to make the palisades between those buildings. Then all we got to do is hang the gates and move in supplies.

"We'll need supplies," said old John Decker more to himself than anyone else.

"The church well is already dug Pa, and as you know, it's got plenty of good water. Cole is forging the gate hinges and Major Starwood has sent his boys yesterday with his sled and oxen to Esopus for four swivel guns we can mount on the walls."

Uncle John looked at the old man sitting in the chair. Old John Decker sipped his toddy. He looked up at his son.

"How about the trees?" he asked.

"Oh Pa, they've been cleared way back just like you wanted. Nobody can get within musket range of the place without us seeing them. Maybe one of them new long-rifles might reach but it wouldn't be no easy shot. Besides the frogs and injuns don't have many long-rifles."

"Good," said the old man.

"By April I want a place where my grandchildren and their friends can get to safety if they need to. I expect you boys to see to it. I expect you all to be ready to help man the walls and do your part. I recon even I might be able to fire one of them swivel guns if I had a boy or two to help me load it."

He winked at Daniel when he said, "We'll give them frogs a surprise if they come round here. Injuns won't want no part of a swivel gun, and they will stay well away from the fort, unless they can put the sneak on us and catch us off guard. That's why I want you boys ready to hit the woods come spring and keep things scouted up. The women folk and children will have to do the Decker planting and field work, this year, I recon."

He took another sip from his cup and listened to the flames and smoke sputtering up the flue.

"The Deckers ain't ever been caught off their guard and we ain't going to be, long as I'm still a-livin'."

People called it Coles Fort because Mr. Cole owned the farm next to the church house. The northwest wall and a good third of the fort sat on his land. Many of the trees used or cleared for the field of fire were his trees. So the name just sort of stuck. But it was a community fort.

The gates were hung on April 10th [20] and the last log of the palisades was sunk into place April 16, 1755. John Decker's family and all the families in this part of the valley now had a place to get to for protection. One of the swivel guns was slightly damaged, when it arrived from Kingston, but all four of them were quickly elevated and mounted on the wall.

The very next morning the swivel guns were test fired to the great satisfaction of everyone present. They had the firm solid sound of cannon. But these weapons were actually much more maneuverable in a close fight. Besides they required far less gunpowder per charge.

---

[20] Approximate date, actual unknown.

Supplies were pouring into the fort from the surrounding farms. But gunpowder as usual was in short supply. More had been requested. It was supposed to be on its way from Morristown. It would travel by ox cart over a new military trail being cut through the mountains from Sussex County's Log Jaol,[21] to Fort John's. War preparations seemed underway everywhere. But nothing was quite complete and no one knew how much time they had before trouble arrived.

Old friends and neighbors looked worried. People were generally quieter now, as if always listening for signs of trouble. Their eyes seemed forever to be scanning the tree lines of nearby fields as if expecting the French or Indians to appear at any moment.

Fort Johns was another new community fort downriver about half way between Machackemack and the Water Gap. It had gotten its name the same way as Cole's fort. It was built on land owned by a man named John Rosecrans.

New Jersey Authorities unlike New York had passed a tax levee raising the necessary resources to support construction and supply for a string of forts along their western frontier. That frontier was mostly made up of the Minisink valley. These forts were finally now being built from the Water Gap to Coles Fort at Machackemack.

New Jersey frontier forts were planned to work in concert with the string of new Pennsylvanian forts. Those forts were also being built now, along the ridges of the Blue Mountains, on a southwest to northeast line terminating at fort Hyndshaw, on the Delaware River, near Shawnee, in Lower Smithfield Township. A Philadelphia printer named Benjamin Franklin had designed those Pennsylvania fortifications and was tasked with getting them constructed as soon as possible.

---

[21] The first county seat for Sussex County New Jersey was simply called Log Jaol. During the war a military trail was built all the way from Elizabethtown the Capital to Fort Johns on the Delaware River.

Nobody believed any of these forts could stop a real army. However, scouts sent out from these strongholds would provide an early warning system and some protection for local folks. At least they would usually hold off small roving bands of savages.

It was mostly these small war parties, which now terrified the entire colonial frontier from Virginia through Pennsylvania. The stories were spreading rapidly northward of whole communities abandoned and farms burned. Other stories were of families murdered, hacked to pieces or drug off into a life of slavery. And then there were the stories of rape, scalping, and various tortures invented or employed by the savages, which caused people to pray for a quick death, when or if, it should come their time to die.

Most families just packed up quick and headed east. But some, who were less afraid or less wise, were determined to stay and defend what they thought rightfully belonged to them.

Protection would depend upon good intelligence. Scouts would be based at these community forts and would perform regular patrols between them. These scouts and spies must stay alive long enough to discover the enemies approach and sound an alarm in time for families to get inside.

Surprisingly, none of the New Yorkers in the Minisink Valley had complained a bit that New Jersey was supporting Coles Fort, as their most northerly base of operation. No one said a word, although the fort clearly sat on land, which many of them had always claimed to be in the colony of New York. If anyone even had such a thought, they kept it to themselves.

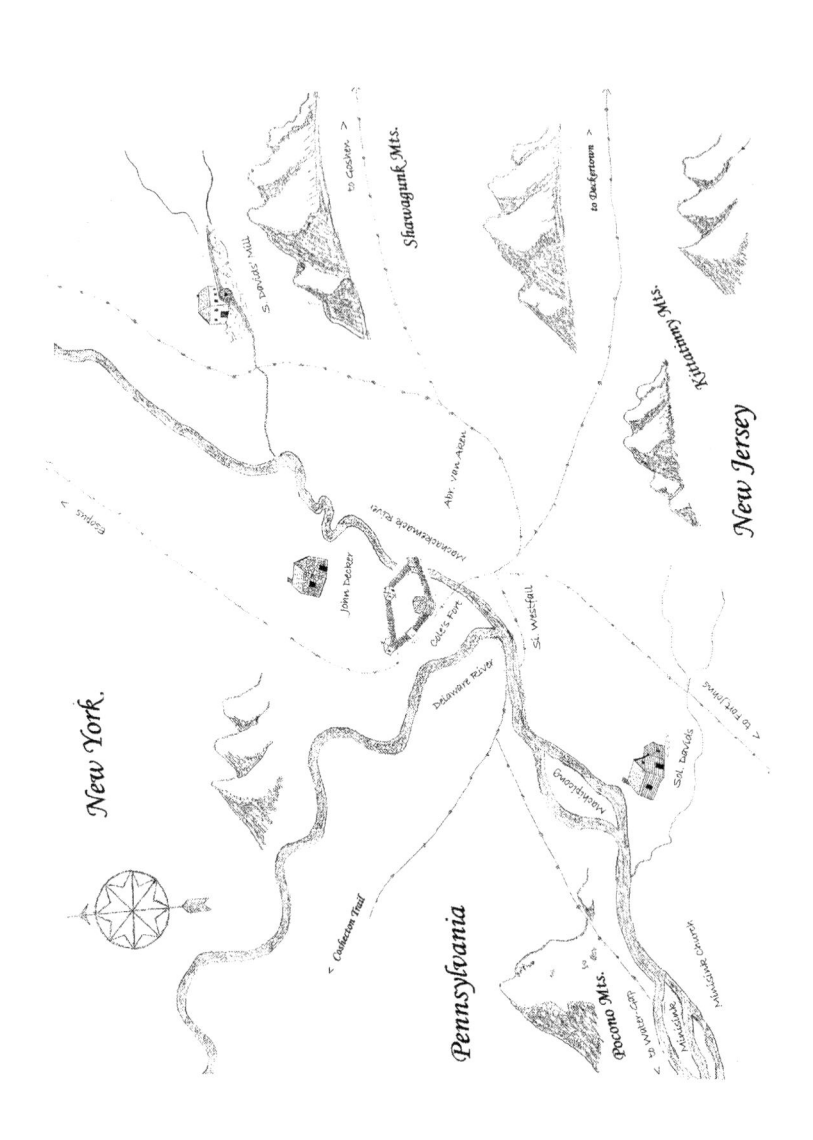

Chapter 27: Gnadenhutten

The dog days of that summer passed slowly with almost no rain. The corn ripened. Small stubby ears drooped on the stalk. Finally the shucks dried and the rich dark brown tassels shivered in the cold November air. The harvest would be sparse.

Lea and Belietje had worked all day yesterday, this morning and half this afternoon. They worked with their brothers Daniel and Jacobus, stripping the gray blades from yellow stalks, binding those stalks into sheaves, and gathering them into shocks. The work had gone well and most of the field, below the barn, stood now in shocks waiting to be hauled to the barn sometime over the winter.

The girls saw Abraham Van Aken ride in and heard his hearty hello. They watched their brothers stop working and saunter over toward the old farmer. The girls could hear him talking but they were too far away to hear what the old man was saying. The cardinals were singing down near the river.

"Boys, I got more news and it's bad again. The Savages hit the Moravians, down at Gnadenhutten, south of lower Smithfield over in Pennsylvania. That's only about 50 miles south of here. Word is they kilt everyone. They was eleven Christian Indians and Missionaries there a week ago. Now they're all dead and the whole place is burned down. Scouts say there might be as many as three or four hundred savages, raiding the countryside over there. Most folks have moved east of the river.

Jacobus and Daniel looked at each other and then back at Mr. Van Aken. Abraham had been their neighbor to the south longer than either of them had been alive. He, Mr. Cole and Pa had bought their farms together and worked the fields the same way, in the early years. He was a good neighbor, which was sometimes almost the same as blood kin. Abraham looked worried.

"Why would they kill the Christian Indians?" asked Daniel.

"I guess it's their way of getting the other Injins to choose sides. I recon they are sending a message. You are either our friend or you're our enemy."

"When?" asked Jacobus looking to the east.

"Four Days ago," the old man said, following the boy's gaze toward the mountain. "There could be hundreds of em' watching us right now."

Slowly he pulled his eyes away from the slope and looked back toward the boys.

"Our family is packin' up and heading to the fort. I expect the alarm will be sent out but even if it isn't we're heading in to fort up, at least for a while. I recon you boys better get your Ma and the children and come in with us. I expect the whole community will be there, for at least a few days; till our scouts can cover some country and have a look see."

Jacobus looked off toward his sisters who were still busy shocking corn. He whistled loudly in their direction. The girls looked up from their work. Jacobus motioned them toward the house and he and Daniel turned toward home, following Mr. Van Aken already riding that way on his horse.

In little more than two hours the Davids and Van Aken families splashed across Machackemack ford rushing their oxen westward up the hill, with two carts full of supplies, and their most valued possessions.

It was the first time eighteen-year-old Belietje Davids ever saw Jacob Fegley. He stood with Andreas Grub and some others just outside the gates at Cole's Fort as she and her family hurried in. She saw the young man following her with his eyes. They were curious, friendly eyes, set in a not unpleasant face. He was dressed in a homespun shirt and deerskin leggings. He had a tomahawk and hunting knife tucked in his belt.

Their eyes met for an instant. Then Belietje looked down and reached out to catch her little brother Petrus, who was stumbling along in front of her. She picked Petrus up and carried him into the fort. As she passed through the gates she wondered: "Is that young stranger still watching me?"

He was, watching her.

"Who's them folks?" he asked Andreas, nodding toward the gate.

"That's the Davids and Van Aken families, from a mile or two north, up Pennhorn road," came the simple answer with a questioning look. "Why?"

"Just wondering."

Within the hour Jacob Fegley was mounted on a spotted horse galloping southward down the KIngs Road toward New Jersey frontier headquarters at Fort Johns some twenty dangerous miles away. The sun was low in the sky and the purple light was dimming. As his horse came up the bank on the east side of Machackemack-Ford he wondered: "Can we cover the five miles to Brinks fort, before sundown?"

Chapter 28: Brink's Fort

*B*rink's Fort was not exactly a community Fort like Cole's Fort. It was really the fortified home of Mathew Brink. But it was supplied and manned, as part of the New Jersey fort system being developed. Jacob Fegley arrived there just before sunset and found Brink and some of his neighbors still working in the days dimming light to improve their fortifications. They were busy placing old fence rails into the cracks between the upright log posts of the palisades. Jacob noticed they were being careful to leave a loop hole every eight or ten posts, which could be opened from the inside, to facilitate their musket fire upon the enemy should it be necessary.

Five families were gathered here tonight along with half a dozen new militiamen who had just arrived, having been officially ordered: "posted at Brinks Fort until further notice".

The main advantage of the little fort was its position near the Kings Road. Sitting upon a small hillock it was surrounded by an open pasture. That grass was normally used for a dozen sheep and a couple milk cows. Brinks Fort was located almost exactly half way between Cole's fort and the new community fort called Nominack being built near Minisink Church. (Jorris David's homestead at Kendiamong was about half way between Brinks and Nominack.)

Jacob planned to spend the night here at Brink's. In the morning he would ride the six miles to Nominack. But the long twelve-mile stretch from Nominack to Headquarters was the part of the ride he dreaded. On the way north he had noted that to be a lonely stretch of road.

He knew another half-way-fort, like Brink's, was being discussed at headquarters, for construction in that area, but none was yet being built. Homesteads on that part of the road were few and far between. That stretch of road would be just the place for the enemy to slip through, or set an ambush. A man on horseback would be a sitting duck. But there was no use thinking about that now.

Jacob hailed the gate was recognized and admitted into Brink's crude little fort. He quickly saw to the care of his horse. Then he sauntered toward one of three fires he saw burning inside the seventy-foot square, picketed enclosure. At this particular fire, five of the six militiamen huddled about, trying to stay warm, toasting themselves first on one side and then on the other. Tonight's cold weather sent smoke shooting straight up, allowing the men to stand close all around the big fire which they kept built tall for the purpose.

The soldiers were a crude talking bunch, mostly young fellows who didn't mean no harm. They had just signed up for the militia pay. Their speech was rough, but they were just farm boys. Mostly they went and did as they were told, just like Jacob.

A pock-faced, young man stepped forward. He looked Jacob up and down but didn't smile.

"I'm Porter Lamb. Who might you be?"

"Jacob Fegley"

"Where you from Jacob Fiiigley?"

Jacob didn't like the way the man mispronounced his name but he had learned long ago to pick his fights carefully. So he answered in a calm voice:

"Paulins-kill a month ago, headquarters two day ago, Coles fort yesterday."

"Where you headin', Back to headquarters?"

"Maybe, unless I decide to go back to Coles Fort. There ain't that many choices."

"No, I recon not, lessen you want to cross the river headin west."

Porter stopped speaking. He stuck his right pinky finger up the left nostril of his large nose and dug for a moment. Then he pulled his finger away to flick something in the dirt and continue:

"But most folks been comin' t'other way if crossin lately. Theys been lots of them folks though, packed light and movin fast as they kin, to get on east of the Kittatinny. Culvers gap is chocked with 'em. I came west through the gap to get here. Counted thirty-three families headin' east, scared to death most of em."

"I used to be enrolled in Colonel McKay's New York militia but my time was up. So I mustered out and came here to show you New Jersey boys how to fight Injins. I can't wait till we can go after them devils. I hear Indian scalps will soon be worth mor'n beaver pelts and their women folk are supposed to become right friendly if you can catch em."

Porter winked at Jacob, and broke into a big buck-toothed grin. Jacob Fegley, began to regret his choice of fires. He said nothing in response to Porter Lamb. Instead he slowly turned to toast his backside. He looked away from the flames out into the star bright sky.

"It sure is a pretty night," he thought.

Chapter 29: Headquarters New Jersey Frontier 1755

Jacob Fegley rode into Fort Johns about one o-clock the next afternoon. His arrival from the north aroused less interest than he had expected.

He noticed a large group of men milling about in the middle of the picketed enclosure. Most of them seemed to be fidgeting with their weapons and other gear. Obviously they were too busy preparing for something else to pay attention to him.

Jacob dismounted. He tied his horse to the hitching post outside the log headquarters building. Then he walked quickly to the open door.

Stepping from the sunlight into the relative darkness of the room, he blinked a couple times and beheld Mr. Edwards at the desk writing rapidly with his quill pen. Two other men, Jacob did not recognize, flanked the fireplace trying not to block the light and still stay warm.

Edwards looked up and then went back to his writing.

"You back already Fegley?" he asked.

"Didn't figure you till toward evening. Did you get your message delivered?"

"Yes sir."

"Have they seen any trouble up that way?"

"No sir, not yet."

Edwards continued his writing.

"Good, you did fine, Jacob. Are you rested up, enough for goin along on a little rescue mission, down into Pennsylvania?"

"I recon so."

"Good, we could use another man. Get your gear checked and ready. We'll be marching by foot to the fort at Walpack and then crossin over the river to Fort Hyndshaw. From there we plan to move on to Dupui's. After that I guess it will depend on what the folks around there need."

He paused and his forehead wrinkled as he re-read what he had written. Then he continued his quick scribbling and said:

"The Frogs and their savages seem to be all over down that way, burnin' and killin' everything they can. People there are forted up or moved east already. Unfortunately a lot of them just didn't move fast enough."

With a flourish, he scribbled a quick signature on his note. He looked up from the paper squarely at Jacob.

"Be ready in one hour."

Edwards looked back down, blotted his original note, pulled another piece of paper from the desk drawer and bent back to his writing.

Jacob backed out of the door into the light of a late November afternoon, wondering what the next few days might bring. Things sure seemed to be happening faster than they used to. Just a month ago, before he joined the militia, his days had seemed to creep along.

Sometimes he lumbered along behind an ox and plow, other times he had stalked deliberately along some faint game trail. Back then the days seemed to drag along with plenty of time.

Now, time was passing more like a blur with him never knowing what might happen next. It was a little scary, but also a bit exciting. He wondered for a fleeting moment what that young, blond gal he had seen at Cole's fort might be doing now.

"She was right pretty," he thought.

Then he remembered where he was heading. He had best see to his gear. He didn't want to forget something. If he were going up against the Indians for the first time he figured he had better be ready.

"I hope we don't run into none," he thought.

Jacob had never fought Indians before. He wasn't sure how he might behave if the savages attacked. It worried him that he might be frightened and just take off running.

Jacob had always enjoyed hunting and living in the woods for weeks. He was good at it too. But the only fighting he had ever done were tussels between boys. As he recalled that fighting wasn't all that much fun even when he won and no one got seriously hurt. The other thing he remembered was that he did not always win.

Fighting with this new enemy he knew would be different. Someone might not always walk away. And that someone might be him.

He knew if he ran from the Indians men like Porter Lamb would brand him a coward. He would probably be hung for desertion. It was a worry. But there was no use thinking about it now. He put it out of his mind and went to his horse.

Chapter 30: Lower Smithfield Township, Northampton County, Pennsylvania

In the gray misty light of dawn, two wooden scows cut wakes across the river. The oarlocks squeaked quietly and the oars splashed a little with each stroke. But those seemed to be the only sounds on the river this morning. Each of the big wooden boats had four men rowing and six others being transported. There was adequate room but it was hard to stay up out of the two inches of water, which for some reason still sloshed about in the bottom of the boat.

Jacob's moccasins were greased.

"They should be waterproof," he thought, "but they weren't intended for wading."

Three mallards suddenly quacked wildly, scudding and flapping their way into quick flight. The bright green heads on two of the birds were clearly visible through the gray mist before they all disappeared into a fog near the Pennsylvania riverbank.

Jacob sat now, frowning, on the edge of the gunnels, keeping his feet elevated and his gear balanced as best he could. He was thinking to himself.

"Any minute now I'm gonna get my feet wet, and that sure ain't going to be good on such a cold day. Or worse yet, if I ain't careful, I'm gonna fall in the darn river and drown. You'd think the captain could have had em bail out a little more water afore we started."

The other men seemed to have their eyes riveted upon the western shoreline. These were the first boats across today and only one man on the far shore scouted that bank for the Pennsylvanians. If he had missed something there could be trouble waiting.

In a few minutes they were across and disembarked. Jacob felt better on dry land and at least his feet were still dry. The wind freshened suddenly blowing the fog off the river.

The boats headed back for their second load, their long oars splashing rapidly. At this rate it would take two more trips, to get their thirty-man company, to the Pennsylvania side of the river. Captain Van-Campin sent a pair of men each, inland one hundred yards, northwest, west and southwest of their position. These men, on picket duty, were to insure the rest of the group waiting beside the river were not surprised. Jacob was sent with a big man named Simon Westfall, to do the picket duty to the northwest.

He and Simon trotted into the brush and quickly covered what they thought was one hundred yards. They were up the bank far enough that Jacob could see out across a little prairie of tall grass, up slope, to a cornfield, which had been cut and shocked. They stopped beside a big sycamore and stood for a moment watching the grass blow to and fro in the breeze.

"There's so much wind today," thought Jacob; "a whole army could be crawling through that grass and we wouldn't know it, until they came out and shot us."

Jacob jumped when Simon tapped him on the shoulder. The big man smiled, with a shrug:

"I'm gonna climb up for a look see."

He leaned his rifle against the sycamore, walked a few paces forward and began climbing a big, scaly riverbirch. The tree had a cluster of three trunks rising close together. Simon worked his way up with his back against one and his feet against another. He was limber for a man his size. Quickly he was high enough to reach the lower limbs. Soon he was up about twenty feet where he stopped and stared off to the northwest.

"Do you see anything?" Jacob asked in a loud whisper.

"No Indians or Frenchies."

"Well, what do you see?"

"A homestead, but the house and barn are all burned up."

"Anyone about?"

"Don't see nothin' movin."

Then Simon turned and looked toward the river.

"I can see the boats goin' back again. They must have just brought over the second load. Won't be long now, they'll be back with the rest of our boys. I got a good view from up here. I'll keep a look out for now, you can take it easy for a while."

"We'll I don't recon I'll be goin' to sleep," said Jacob as he sat down, on a nearby log, and laid his musket across his knees. His eyes still watched the nearby grassland. He knew if there was anyone laying out there, Simon might not see them until it was too late.

Time seemed to slow again. Minutes passed like hours. Jacob did not like picket duty. It left too much time for thoughts he did not want to have: Would he stand and fight when he needed to? When was it acceptable and smart to run away? How would it feel to be shot? Did Indians scalp you if you were only wounded? All these things were running through his mind as he watched the grass.

He heard Simon moving. He looked up to see the man climbing down.

"Do you see something coming?" Jacob whispered.

"Yes." Simon said, as he jumped, the last six feet to the ground. He landed like a cat, on all four in perfect balance, stood and strode the few steps necessary to grab his weapon.

"Where?" asked Jacob.

"There!" said Simon with a smile.

He was pointing toward the river. Jacob could see one of their own company coming toward them. It was the man Jacob knew as Groundhog approaching them through the woods.

"See anything boys?" asked Groundhog in a hushed voice.

"Nothin but a burned out farm," said Simon.

"Well, the captain says we're moving out, down the trail that is just up the slope a bit. He wants you two to come along but stay behind us about this same distance watching the rear. If you see anything way back, come up quick and quiet to let us know. If their close behind, and likely to surprise us, get off a warning shot and come a runnin, if you can, or hide in the brush, if you have to. Do you understand?

"Yeah. We understand," said Jacob, "but we don't like it."

"Well you can take that up with the captain ifin you want to. But I wouldn't advise it," said Groundhog.

"He gets a little touchy 'bout fellers questioning his orders and he don't look to happy today no-how. That scout they sent us from Fort Hyndshaw says most of the farms 'tween here and the fort are burnt up or abandoned. So don't be expectin' no biscuits and jam. I got to get back. The captain says we move when I tell him you fellers are watching the rear. Good luck."

Groundhog scurried off, the way he had come. As he moved away through the woods, Jacob thought he had an idea how Groundhog might have gotten his name.

Chapter 31: March to Dupui's

Rear guard duty was new to Simon Westfall and Jacob Fegley. In fact soldiering itself was new. This was really the first mission where either man actually expected he might encounter the enemy.

Quickly they learned that it took some getting used to. It was hard to monitor what was happening to the rear when you were busy trying not to fall behind the company, which was moving rapidly away from you. And the only thing either man was absolutely sure about was that he did not want to be left behind.

Soon they passed another abandoned farm. This time the buildings stood, but there was a strange stillness about them. Jacob half expected to see them burst into flames as he walked past. Looking backward over his shoulder he kept watching. But the buildings didn't catch fire. They just stood forlornly. Then they faded away into the distance behind to await their uncertain fate.

An hour later Jacob and Simon first saw Fort Hyndshaw across a large meadow. It was a small fort, set to the left of the trail, closer to the river. As they watched it the stockade gates opened. Five of the defenders rushed out at the quick step to join their own company marching ahead, proceeding southward along the trail.

When Jacob and Simon walked past the fort, a sentry on the wall waved his hat in a slow arc above his head and they returned his salute. The fort was too far away from the trail for any words to pass between them without shouting. Shouting just didn't seem appropriate this morning. They trotted on, with a few glances rearward to be sure nobody was slipping up from behind. The track to the rear seemed empty.

In another mile or two Simon and Jacob had developed their own system for doing rear guard. For a few paces Jacob walked slowly backward watching the rear. Then he turned and began trotting to catch up. When Simon heard Jacob start trotting he turned, walked backward and watch behind as Jacob trotted up and past him. After Simon heard Jacob stop trotting he turned again... In this leapfrog fashion one of them was always looking back, while the other was catching up and watching forward.

During the morning they passed half a dozen other abandoned farms. All had their houses burned, some their barns too.

Occasionally Jacob and Simon would lose sight of the company, around a curve, over a hill or down a quick slope. At these times a strange lonesomeness quickly settled over Jacob. At such times he noticed a new quickness in his movements. His senses were suddenly more acute. Every sound caught his attention. Then the column would reappear, sometimes further off, but more often too near for the correct performance of their rear guard duty. They were supposed to be guarding the rear of the column, not catching up to it.

Rear guard was not especially hard, but it did require an aggressive focus. Jacob knew it was a big responsibility. He was aware also of its dangers.

"It would be easy enough to kill us back here," he thought

"Especially when we are out of sight. If we didn't get off a shot the captain wouldn't even know we were dead, until the enemy slipped up and killed half of the company."

Jacob did not like being out of sight of the militia troop. He promised himself he would remain alert and ready. But secretly, Jacob hoped he and Simon would not be left on this duty long. He liked it better marching with the men; unless, of course, he could be mounted on a fast horse.

He looked ahead at Westfall, who was presently walking backward facing him as he was trotted forward.

"I wonder how he feels about this job?" thought Jacob. But he did not ask, and he could not tell.

Simon Westfall seemed alert. His movements were neither slow nor quick. He had a smooth easy way. Simon's eyes always appeared to be scanning far off. But Jacob noticed that Simon never missed place a step, never tripped, never stumbled. Simon looked at home on the trail but he had said little, since leaving the river.

Jacob began to think maybe Simon Westfall might be a good companion. In the backcountry the choice of companions could often be the most important decision a man might make. Jacob believed firmly that bad companions, sooner or later, always brought bad luck. He was determined in his life to choose wisely, when he had the choice.

"If I have to be assigned this duty," he thought, "at least, maybe, I'm doing it with a man I can trust. Time will tell."

Sometime before noon, as Simon was trotting up to catch Jacob, the big man pointed forward:

"Here comes Groundhog."

Jacob stopped and they stood together. Simon watched the runner come hustling up the trail toward them while Jacob continued watching the rear. Soon, Groundhog trotted up wheezing from his effort.

"Trouble ahead," he said. He paused, catching his breath.

"A father and three youngins…all dead. No sign of anyone else. Captain figures the mother and maybe couple children may have been drug off. God help 'em. We're stopping to bury the dead. Won't take long. We got to move fast."

He paused to breathe again.

"We're only about three miles out from Dupui's. They probably don't even know about these folks. Likely killed this morning."

He looked off apprehensively, to the right and left, into the woods. Again nothing seemed to catch his attention.

"They must have thought they were safe this close to the fort. They were sure wrong about that. Some folks just won't face facts till it's too late. If they were lucky we'll find the rest of the family at Dupui's. But the sign we're reading says otherwise.

Captain is sending five men to track the war party. Unlikely they'll catch em. You boys keep a sharp watch. I'll signal with a wave when we are ready to move. You signal back so I know you see me. Do you understand?"

"Yes," said Simon as he moved to the side of the trail taking a seat on a large boulder.

Groundhog turned and scurried back to join the company. Simon looked at Jacob. Jacob was looking back with a strange appearance. Simon had seen that expression before when folks were about ready to lose their breakfast.

"Happy to be back here, now," said Simon. "Don't care to be diggin bury holes, or seeing what the boys are lookin at."

He looked back up the trail they had just traveled. His eyes studied every nearby tree and bush. Then he gazed past all that, as far as he could see, into the cold, foreboding, November forests surrounding them.

Jacob settled down on a nearby rock. He said nothing but his eyes too were busy scanning the deep woods around them for any sign of movement.

Chapter 32: The Broadhead Rescue

About two o'clock in the afternoon, the company reached Dupui's. By the time Jacob and Simon came in the gate the rumor was already among the men—they weren't staying. Each of the men hastily gathered around and got a few spoonfuls of stew, from a common pot, cooking on a big fire. Then a man came forward pouring rum into your cup, if you had a cup. Jacob and Simon both did. By the time all that was done the captain was standing on a stump.

"Boys, we're movin on. Southwest of here is a man named Daniel Broadhead. His family and three other families are holed up at his place. We're goin to escort them back here. There has been trouble down that way. We may need to bury some more folks along the way, but we're goin. We'll head out in five minutes. If anyone needs supply see Mr. Dupui, but do it quick!"

In five minutes the company moved. There were no complaints. Each man seemed lost in his own thoughts but they moved as a unit, on a clear mission they all understood. Jacob and Simon were still on the rear guard; but neither man thought about asking the captain for a new assignment.

The rest of the afternoon passed slowly as they marched to the southwest, over rough rocky trail. They passed one homestead and then another. They stopped to bury the dead at some farms. All the plantations had the homes burned. Jacob got used to seeing piles of black charred debris, with fireplace chimneys, rising as stark, lonely, spires, toward the gray overcast sky.

While they were waiting at one homestead to bury the dead, Groundhog came scurrying back after they had been stopped for a short while. He wasn't moving fast this time. He came on carefully, carrying a small wooden pail.

"Brought you boys some milk," he said.

"Little Jersey cow came in from the woods. Her udders were all swollen and dripping. She needed milkin' real bad. One of the boys took care of her. I thought I'd bring you a bit. It's a sad task, the boys figure she's likely never been milked by anyone but the misses and kids we're a-buryin'.

I recon she'll come along with us now. We sure as the devil ain't goin' to leave her to the savages."

Simon and Jacob pulled out their cups and Groundhog poured them full. The milk was still warm as they drank. It tasted good—thick and creamy.

Before dusk the company reached Broadhead's, although Jacob and Simon never saw the place up close. Groundhog came back again, this time carrying only orders.

"Captain says for you boys to take up a position a bit further off. Give warnin' if you see anything. We'll be packin' up these folks quick as we can. Got to round up some livestock. Then we'll be movin' after dark back to Dupui's. Personally, I cain't wait till we get back across the Delaware, where we belong. Over on this side the Injins still figure it's their land."

"We're kinda exposed here," said Simon. "We'll move back another fifty yards. I noticed a little game track back there a-ways, where we can get off to the side of the main trail. We'll give you a warning shot if needed. Okay?"

"Okay," said Groundhog.

He scurried off. Jacob noted once more that the heavy man moved resembling his namesake, with quick steps on short legs. But Jacob noted also that there was a grace to the movements. Groundhog blended into the surroundings quickly.

Jacob and Simon soon retraced their steps. Turning right along the game trail they continued for forty paces and then right again, about thirty paces up a little slope. They settled behind a large rock, beside some laurel bushes, in a very good natural blind. From here, they could watch down the road they had come in on and also along the game trail, which crossed it.

Jacob noticed Simon raise the frizzen and check the black-powder priming in the flash-pan of his musket. Quickly, he did likewise. Then they each settled in for the wait leaning against the large rock, one looking out from each side.

It was a naturally camouflaged position. Each man had set themselves along many a game trail just like this. But the wild game they sought today was more wary and dangerous than either had ever hunted before.

Today's light was fading fast. A blue jay suddenly screamed his last call of the day and winged his way off through the forest. Squirrels stopped digging in the dry leaves and scurried off toward nests higher among the bare limbs of the tall beech trees. Somewhere in the distance a barred owl began its haunting call.

The woods were quieting. Jacob pulled his hat down tighter. In a few minutes it was colder and darker.

Jacob felt Simon nudge him very slowly in the ribs. They were well hidden behind the rock. Jacob moved his head quietly, almost imperceptibly to his left. He knew Simon had seen something. Jacob saw nothing, except tree trunks, laurel branches, and a few tall, thin, beech-saplings, reaching for the light of next summer's sky.

Then he saw it—or them—there were two.

Instantly, he knew they were savages. They were stalking warily along the game trail, taking a few silent steps each, then both pausing at once to watch and listen. They moved as gracefully as any buck or doe. They made no sound to betray themselves.

"I wonder if they can smell us as well as white tail do?" thought Jacob. Then he felt the wind in his face. "Even if they were deer, we should be okay," he thought. "They wouldn't smell us till they're close enough for it to be too late."

The savages paused a long time in the shadows where the trail crossed the road. Then they trotted silently overand into the woods on this side. They were close. But not yet close enough.

Jacob knew where the shot was. It was directly in front of him, after the savages passed the rock, behind which he and Simon hid. The Indians would be looking ahead for danger, not off to their right and slightly behind. It was the perfect ambush. He had no doubt that Simon saw all that as clearly as he did. They had to wait but a few seconds more.

It was nearing dark now and the only detail Jacob could see on the two apparitions coming toward him were the two feathers tied in their hair. The feathers palpitated leaf-like in the cold breeze. Jacob knew this foe was a dangerous one. His heart pounded like a drum in his chest. His palms began to sweat.

"Thank god for this rock," he thought.

The savages passed momentarily out of his vision behind some laurel bushes. He raised his riffle. He had already pulled the hammer back. Now they waited. It seemed like an abnormally long pause the savages had taken behind the Laurel.

Jacob began to worry. "Maybe they sense trouble. Will they pass by the clear shot moving, or stop and pause? Either way it's a shot of forty paces. How can we miss."

Jacob had seen the handiwork of savages all day long. He knew the enemy. These two were about to pay for all the bad deeds he had witnessed today.

The two Indians were moving at a slow trot when they entered the firing zone. From behind the rock, both muskets flashed and roared, shattering the stillness of the evening. When the powder smoke cleared Jacob was astonished by what he saw.

The second savage was on the ground out in front of them on the trail. He was not making a sound, but his leg thrashed wildly in the leaves. Then the leg slowed, twitched a few more times and grew still.

But there was no sign of the other savage. The one Jacob had aimed at—was gone.

The forest was silent. Neither Jacob nor Simon moved. Both listened intently, trying desperately to sense from where the danger might come next. Both quietly reloaded their rifles, but then sat tight, covered and concealed by the growing darkness. They knew better than to move to soon. They listened for ten minutes more, hearing nothing. It was completely dark now. They heard a twig snap. Someone was coming along the road.

"Is that you Groundhog?" asked Simon in a voice only slightly louder than a whisper.

"Yeah," came the reply, "and I got a few of the boys with me."

"Well, watch yourselves, there may be at least one still out there somewhere. We got another here on the trail ahead of us. He ain't moved since right after we fired, so I'm saying he's dead. We'll check him and meet you at the road. Don't shoot us coming out."

"Okay, come on."

Simon and Jacob stalked slowly and quietly, their rifles at the ready toward the body on the trail. In the dim starlight Simon poked the body hard with his musket to be sure there was no life left. The body lay still.

In this darkness, there was no way to see much, except by feel. Simon searched the body and Jacob studied the trail where his adversary had escaped.

"Surly I hit him," thought Jacob. He bent down low feeling with one hand along the trail in the dry leaves for signs of blood. He felt nothing that was wet or sticky. He had missed. But for the life of him he could not see how.

"I got what I need," said Simon. "Let's get."

With that the two of them walked cautiously toward the road.

"We're coming out," said Simon. "Don't shoot us."

"Come on," whispered Groundhog. "We ain't gonna shoot."

Chapter 33: Back to Dupui's

The fortified home of Samuel Dupui was better supplied than some forts Jacob Fegley had seen during his short time in the frontier militia. There were no cannon or swivel guns.

But Jacob had noted yesterday, that they did have plenty of other stuff: things like gun-powder, muskets, blankets, pistols, flints, wool cloth, and even oiled canvas to keep off the rain. And he saw plenty of food too: apples and raisins and dried peaches, just to name a few. Hams and haunches of venison or beef hung inside and out. And taters, pumpkins and squash were heaped in wooden bins and piled high in corners.

Dupui was a trader. He knew how to keep himself supplied and he had a big market. Most of the families now fleeing east, or dying in the Pennsylvania wilderness, had resupplied from time to time at Samuel Dupui's.

Jacob was looking forward to getting back to Dupui's place before breakfast. Little sign of any light showed now in the East. It was the time of the beaver moon but that yellow globe hung low in the western sky. It kept hiding its light for long stretches behind clouds which kept rolling in from the west. But the moon did peak out, from time to time. When it did the bare trees stood out starkly black against the November night sky.

A cold wind began whipping Jacobs face. He stopped walking long enough to pull a wool scarf from his possible-bag and wrap it around his neck. Instantly he felt warmer.

"I think that's snow I smell," he thought.

The company had not left Broadhead's till almost three o'clock in the morning. Moving four families with all the livestock, which could be rounded up in the dark, proved troublesome. But, so far no sign of any more Indians or Frenchmen.

"At least on the return trip we've not had to bury any families," thought Jacob.

"It's been near twenty-four hours since I've slept or had anything much to eat. I wonder if they'll have eggs at the fort?"

Jacob thought he saw just the beginning of some light, just now, in the eastern sky. He and Simon Westfall had been on rear guard during this night march too. In the darkness they followed only fifty yards behind the men driving the livestock. They had no trouble keeping up and with all the noise of the present company there was no worry about getting lost.

Two wagons, four horses, seventy-three human beings, half a dozen cows (with all the cow-bells removed), eight sheep and two goats, make quite a disturbance moving along a nighttime road. No matter how quiet they try to be.

The captain sent out scouts and flankers, as well as a rear guard to listen and watch for approaching danger. Ambush was the fear. Those thoughts troubled Jacob.

"We're close to the fort now," he thought.

"Just when we might be letting down our guard, feeling safe. Just when I would attack if I were the enemy."

Sparrows chirped in the meadow ahead. The gray light of morning was here now. The familiar black hulking shape of the Kittatinny Mountains beckoned to Jacob from a few miles away, across the river.

He watched the cattle being driven ahead. He saw beyond the cattle to the wagons flanked by the women and children, trudging along with their heads down at the front of the company. He could not yet see the fort but he knew it was up there. He visualized the scouts arriving before the gates and the gates being swung open, wide, to admit the tired and frightened pilgrims.

Immediately Jacob strained to see in every direction. He saw an empty road behind him with late November forests spreading out on either side. A Jay began to scream in the distance.

When he turned back to the front, tall brown grass, rippled in the meadow, and the fort stood suddenly visible, through the fog, its gates open. The pilgrims were entering and the oxen plodded slowly along with swaying heads and tails flicking side to side.

Jacob Fegley smelled fresh manure and then, he caught a whiff of something else—wood-smoke and frying pork. Instantly his stomach began to growl.

"I hope they got eggs," he thought.

A week later the company was back across the Delaware River to New Jersey Frontier Headquarters at Fort Johns. A dusting of snow had fallen. The air was cold enough to start freezing not just in buckets and troughs but also along the edges of fast moving streams. The captain was inside sitting warm at his crude desk before the fireplace scribbling away with his quill. Most of his militiamen were outside lounging beside their cook-fires. Winter was going to arrive soon with some serious weather.

Jacob Fegley strolled up to one of those fires. He was just returning from the hostlers. He had requested the horse he would need for another ride north. He was being sent back to Cole's fort, this time for the winter.

Five other militiamen had been sent ahead of him before he and the company had returned from Dupui's. Jacob would carry instructions and reports north and join this squad. Their little troop would constitute the official New Jersey militia presence at Coles Fort. He had no idea what that duty might be like.

Jacob would not be riding north alone. Simon Westfall was going with him, but not as a militiaman. It turned out that Simon had been along on the mission into Pennsylvania only as a private citizen. The big frontiersman, Jacob had learned, owned a substantial farmstead near carpenters point. He was going home to his family.

As Jacob approached the cook-fire, he thought about the shot he had missed, that evening near Broadhead's cabin. Nobody spoke as he walked up to the fire. Everyone seemed talked out a week after their mission had ended.

A tall soldier sat on a stump mending his moccasin. His bare foot rested on a log in front of the fire. Another soldier, who Jacob knew only as Wilson, roasted three strips of bacon over a long forked stick, which he had just cut and shaved the bark from. Groundhog snored with a wet sputter next to the fire. He slept sitting upright, his back resting on a small sapling, which for some reason had been left growing inside the newly picketed compound. It was a restful morning.

"How could I have missed?" Jacob wondered to himself. It was a question he could not get out of his mind. "Did I forget to load a ball?"

Jacob had known of men who had mistakenly rammed down a second cleaning patch on top of a powder charge, instead of a ball-in-a-patch.

"I've never done that before. But then, I never missed a shot of forty paces at such a large target moving so slowly."

It was a puzzle he just couldn't explain. And he could not forget about it either.

To his credit Simon Westfall had never mentioned the missed shot. He was, after all, the only witness unless you counted the savage who yet roamed free because of Jacobs's poor aim. If Simon wondered about it he did not let it show. But Jacob could think of little else.

He watched Wilson roast the bacon. Grease dripped into the coals caused the flame to reach higher and higher. The forked stick was smoking now. In another second it would be a-blaze.

"Close enough!" Wilson finally exclaimed, tossing the bacon onto a thick slice of bread he had waiting.

"Could I have pulled my shot in the excitement?" Jacob wondered.

"I don't think I was that frightened."

"I never killed a man before. Maybe I just didn't want to do it."

"Naw, I wanted to, plenty!"

"Will I miss next time?"

"I better not, or next time they may get me."

※

Inside Headquarters the captain penned his final report:

"The Barbarous and bloody scene which is now open in the above place (Lower Smithfield Township Northampton County Pennsylvania) is the most lamentable that perhaps has ever appeared. There is no person possessed of any humanity but would commiserate the deplorable fate of these unhappy people. There may be seen horror and desolation, populous settlements deserted, villages laid under ashes, men, women, and children, cruelly mangled and massacred, some found in the woods very nauseous for want of interment, some just reeking from the hands of their savage slaughters, and some hacked and covered all over with wounds." (Hillman, 1934)

The captain rose from his chair, stepped to the fireplace, coughed and spat into the flames. He returned to sit at his desk. Picking up his quill he wrote:

"Samuel Dupui seems to be very near being in the same deplorable situation, and will unavoidably share the same fate with his neighbors. On his applying to Mr. Stewart and myself, we raised a fine rifle company and went to his assistance, and when

we arrived there, we were informed that Broadhead's, which is about five miles further down, was surrounded and besieged by the Indians, Upon which we marched to his relief and escorted him and his effects to the Delaware, with what cattle and effects we could find in the night." (Hillman, 1934)

The captain looked up toward the rafters, at the underside of the shake roof. The building was well constructed, he thought considering its' having been built so hastily. He looked back to his paper and wrote:

"We continued there abouts four days, and all the while heard nothing but outcries and alarms, and our sentries were fired upon by some Indians hovering around Dupui's home, which may be deemed a sure prognostic of it's destruction." (Hillman, 1934)

The captain looked up again, briefly, watching the shadows reflected from the flames dancing among the rafters like ghosts, then he looked back to his paper and scribbled a post script, attaching a list of the forty homes that had been burned and the eighty-nine people who were brutally killed by the savages.

Back near Broadhead's cabin, in Pennsylvania, the snow fell hard and fast. The woods were quiet, save for the wind howling and blowing the snowflakes into drifts, here and there, upon the forest floor. The cabin nearby stood as it had the night it was abandoned. No other human beings had disturbed the quiet here since that time.

Today, the track of a single man showed in the trail leading toward the cabin. The impressions in the snow had come out of the forest onto the pathway a quarter mile before, but were quickly filling. Soon they would disappear beneath the blowing snow. As the tracks approached the cabin they turned left along a small game trail. Here the fresh footprints were cut deep and here stood an Indian warrior motionless, staring into the forest.

His tired face, painted with black and red streaks, stood out starkly, if less fiercely on this morning, set against the cold whiteness. In the crook of his arm balanced an ancient musket with aged leather strapping wrapped about the wooden stock—old repairs. He wore deerskins with a faded red blanket slung over his shoulders as a cloak. A single eagle feather, secured loosely by a leather string, hung in his hair.

The feather and a few strands of his own long black hair quivered in the wind. So also did a tuft of blond hair, attached to a scalplock, hanging from his belt. Otherwise he did not stir. He stared into the woods, slowly scanning the area with his eyes.

Suddenly a look of understanding settled upon his tired face. He strode strait-way toward a large boulder some forty paces up slope. He stopped half way there. Immediately before him was a small beech sapling. Its one inch diameter trunk was bent double about three feet up from the earth. Today's' snow and wind had caused the top of the tree to lay over now upon the ground.

He reached out his right hand to lift up the small tree. He could see clearly where half the wood had been ripped away on the left side of the tiny tree trunk. He let it fall and watched the hanging snow drop from its branches.

Now, Otter understood what had happened. It was clear to him that the ambush had come from the bolder above. The enemy had remained concealed until he and Painted Turtle had passed, and then they had fired upon them. It was a good ambush. It should have worked.

Otter knew that he was alive today only because Manitou had grown this little tree to take the bullet intended for him. That bullet, when it struck the tree, had been sent careening off to the left and had missed its intended destination in his heart. He did not yet know why he had been spared but Manitou would no doubt reveal that to him at some later time.

For now he must bury the lifeless body of his friend, who lay covered in snow, on the game trail behind him. He looked about for rocks and brush. The snow was falling so hard it was difficult to see far.

There was a bite to the wind. It would take time. The ground was frozen. There was no other way. He would do the best he could for his friend but he needed to do it quickly.

The rest of the war party was well ahead of Otter, heading west over the mountains. It was a long way to the Wyoming Valley. According to signs provided by The Father-of-life, Otter suspected winter this year, would be long and hard. Come spring they would return to finish what they had begun.

Chapter 34: Christmas 1755

Just two days until Christmas, yet so far, winter had been mild. It was cold. The ground was frozen. But there was only an inch of snow cover, except where the wind blew steadily, and there large patches of frozen earth still lay exposed.

Belietje Davids stepped from the church doorway into the quiet of the stockade grounds at Cole's Fort. Carefully she adjusted her wool scarf, to cover not only her neck but her lower chin as well. There were only a handful of people in sight. Most of the community had returned to their homes. The recent fear of Indian attack had subsided.

She looked with interest across the parade grounds, past the gate, toward the blockhouse. She knew the little New Jersey militia troupe of six was billeted there for the winter. But today she saw none of them about.

Belietje wondered where Jacob Fegley might be today. She had been introduced to the man in church the week before. Simon Westfall had come home with the young militiaman, following their rescue mission down into Lower Smithfield Township, North Hampton County, Pennsylvania.

Simon was introducing Jacob lately to all the local families. He seemed to be introducing Jacob not as just another New Jersey militiaman, sent to fight Indians, but as a new best friend. The two had become quite close during their short acquaintance.

Belietje was not so quick to make judgments about people. She was willing to accept Jacob to Sunday services on Simon's recommendation, but she would reserve her own personal judgment about the man, at least for a while yet, she reckoned. Still the boy was friendly and he seemed to have an unusually keen interest in her.

Jacob Fegley seemed backward, or bashful but not stupid. He made no attempt to speak directly to Belietje, except when Simon made the formal introduction. Even then Jacob had said simply "pleased to meet you miss". But Belietje had caught the young man several times, from a distance watching her.

He had a distinctly German accent, like most folks who came from over the mountains, from the valley of the Paulinskill. She noticed also that Jacob possessed a pleasant, honest smile. He also seemed to have all his own teeth. That was more than some men his age could offer a gal.

Sister Lea and Daniel suddenly popped out the doorway behind her, disturbing her thoughts.

"Ready to go sis?" asked Daniel.

"Yes," said Belietje. "Let's get; it's almost noon, and those, clouds look like they've got snow in em."

Together the three teenagers strode off, at a quick pace, toward the gate. As they neared the entrance Jacob Fegley came galloping in on a sorrel horse. The animal was sweating through its thick winter-coat despite the cold temperatures. Quickly Jacob drew rein, halting his mount with warm breath steaming from its nostrils and hooves still clattering and dancing on the frozen ground.

"Good Day Miss Davids," said Jacob touching a mittened right hand to his hat and dipping his head just a bit. Then before anyone could answer he loosed his rein, leaned forward in the saddle, and trotted his horse away toward the blockhouse. Lea and Daniel gawked at Belietje, each with a big toothy grin.

"He weren't lookin' at me when he said that!" said Lea.

Belietje, who had stopped walking when Jacob spoke, was standing now with her mouth slightly agape. She yanked her scarf up close around her nose and hurried on out the gate. But she had not covered her face before Lea noticed a new rosiness in her sister's cheeks.

Lea cast a questioning glance toward Daniel. He gazed back, with a twinkle in his eye. He shrugged his shoulders in answer. Then they both rushed off hurrying to catch up to their sister.

Chapter 35: Susquehanna Hunt

Winter 1755, was hard for the Munsi living in the Susquehanna country. They had lived here 18 summers, but it still was not home. The old ones longed for the ancestral village on the Fishkill.

Even the young, yearned for those ancient magical lands, told of by their elders: mountain coves and river islands, where winter was warmer and summer cooler; hills and streams, where hunting and fishing was easy; river bottom soils, where the three sisters of corn, beans and squash lived happy and grew best; land stolen, through fraud, by Pennsylvanians; fields farmed now by Connecticut strangers, and some by old friends of the Munsi, who had moved across the big river, to squat on property, rightfully belonging to "The People".

But, Manitou had seen the wrong. He had sent Frenchmen to supply muskets and gunpowder. The French had even brought soldiers of their own from Quebec, with cannon. The Munsi had helped these Frenchmen defeat the British and Virginians, in the Ohio country, not only once, but twice, in the past two summers. Many scalps had been taken along with much plunder.

Then winter had come. It had been long. It was now a time of great cold; a time of breaking bones for the marrow and very thin soup.

"The winter has been difficult," thought Otter as he gathered wood in the snowy forest. "But, the Father-of-life no longer smiles on the Pennsylvanians. Many of them suffer also."

Otter had been forced to walk a distance to find this wood. Now he was returning to the hunting camp, situated in a tiny cove of pine trees, just down the slope. In the distance, he could see that Red-corn had been successful with the flint and steel. A small fire was already ablaze. Its tiny dancing flame was a welcome sight as the sunlight faded on this cold day.

The hunting had been hard. But his party had two small deer carcasses, tied now, to an improvised sled. Otter, Red-corn, Twisted-stalk and the Frenchman named Lafollette had been out for six days on this hunt. Tomorrow they would return to the village, and some of the old ones and the children would eat meat for the first time in several weeks.

As he neared camp Otter could see Lafollette and Twisted-stalk walking in, to his right and left. They were also coming from up the slope. Twisted-stalk carried a small load of wood but Lafollette was dragging a large deadfall, which would have been too big without the help of the downward momentum.

The three wood gatherers reached camp about the same time and threw all the wood into a pile. Without a word, each man rolled out his own bedroll, laying it in the snow, close around the fire.

The Munsi bedrolls were of elk hide, with the inside of the skin turned outward and greased heavily with bear grease. The warm, soft, furry side faced inward.

Lofollette's bedroll consisted of a well-greased piece of canvas and a heavy wool capote. Sometimes, on cold days he wore the capote as a cloak. Each man would sleep warm so long as the night were not too cold and they remained close to the fire.

Later, Otter swallowed his last bite of tenderloin, fresh roasted from the coals. He licked the grease from his fingers, smacking his lips, wiped his hands on his breeches, patted his stomach three times, and belched.

It was dark now. Tonight there was no moon. Twisted-stalk rose and began breaking sticks and tossing them onto the coals of their cook-fire. Then, the hunters sat on their bedrolls enjoying the warmth of their re-kindled flames.

Lofollette produced a clay pipe from his duffel. Then he began rummaging about in his pack looking for tobacco.

The wind had died down. It was beginning to snow again.

"In spring, thousands of French soldiers and friendly Indians will sweep down from Montreal, as many as the geese last fall. They will destroy the English in Albany. Any who stand with the English will be destroyed as well," said Lafollette.

He found the tobacco pouch. Carefully he untied it and began filling the pipe. With his thumb, he deliberately packed, each little bit, of the dried, crumbled leaf down into the bowl. It was important in this sacred ritual not to waste any of the valued tobacco. He spoke slowly and clearly as he continued.

"This summer, the Munsi will regain their homeland and punish the Pennsylvanians. Any who stand with the Pennsylvanians will also be our enemy."

He picked up a small stick from the fire, holding the burning brand to the bowl of the pipe. Drawing slowly through the stem he lit the tobacco.

From out in the darkness, the men heard the short howls of a wolf pack gathering for a hunt. Twisted-stalk smiled at his friend Red-corn and nodded toward the familiar sounds.

"The Iroquois, who fight for the English, will be busy in the North," said Lafollette. "Huron and more Frenchmen will be sent to help us in our fight. But the cannon will be needed elsewhere."

He passed the pipe to Otter who received it respectfully. Otter put the stem to his mouth drawing in the smoke from the pipe while watching the campfire.

Temporarily the flames seemed to leap even higher, casting strange shadows upon the nearby trees. Somewhere in the darkness the wolf pack silently closed in upon their prey as the men listened in anticipation.

After a few, slow, thoughtful puffs from the pipe, Otter turned to look at the Frenchman and asked, "how does Lafollette know the plans of the French Commanders—so far away?"

Lafollette turned, toward Otter. The earnest countenance on his bearded face was clearly displayed in the firelight.

"The currier, who came to visit before the deep snow, left me the orders. There are spies everywhere and it was not wise to tell too much. The snow will melt soon and we will need to be ready. I will tell the village when we arrive. If the other hunting parties have done well, we will feast."

Otter thought about what had been said and leaned over to pass the pipe around the flames to Red-corn.

"It is good," Otter said to Lafollette. Then, looking across the fire at his friends, he added, "Tobacco-spit will be very angry."

Their old friend, Tobacco-spit, had badly broken a leg last summer during the Battle of Monongahela. It had healed crooked. He could hardly walk. To make things worse, Tobacco-spit had fallen through the ice in early winter. He had suffered greatly from the cold ever since. He would not be able to take up the warpath this year, or maybe ever again.

"Tobacco-spit hates Pennsylvanians. It will make him very angry to be left behind," Otter explained to Lafollette.

What he didn't say, but what Otter thought to himself, was that their old friend Big-nose would be sorry to miss this fight too. Big-nose had never been happy, hunting in the Susquehanna country. It had made him very angry to be forced to leave his home on Minisink Island.

Ten summers ago he had gone alone on a long hunt back to the Fishkill. He had not returned.

When Big-nose did not come back to his home on the Susquehanna Otter led a search party to the headwaters of the Ramondskill. They saw many things, but they found no sign of their friend. They returned to tell June-bug that she was now a widow.

"Maybe soon," Otter said, "all Munsi people will return forever to their homeland—to live and die."

Somewhere out in the darkness, a rabbit's scream was suddenly cut short, and in the silence, which followed, the campfire crackled.

Early that spring Munsi women went looking for the bloodroot plant. They found it growing on the forest floor, its small, delicate, white flowers some of the first in bloom. They dug the plants and returned to their wigwams and cabins[22].

With care the women of the tribe drained the sap from the roots of the bloodroot, mixing it with tallow, as they sang an ancient prayer. Otter, Twisted-stalk, Red-corn and hundreds of other warriors in the Munsi tribe sang other chants. Solemnly the warriors adorned their faces with the red paint of the bloodroot.

The Munsi had been wronged. Their land had been taken by Fraud. White men had done the deed using the Iroquois to enforce the order. It did not matter that the men responsible were far away. Someone in that tribe would have to pay.

The Delaware warriors took up their weapons heading south and east in small roving bands. Otter joined Lafollette, in the first war party heading south.

A short time later, Twisted-stalk and Red-corn joined a war party of twelve heading east, crossing the Poconos.

After a few grueling days traversing undulating mountain trails, seemingly always with more up than down, Red-corn and Twisted-stalk's war party crested yet another ridge. Then they began another decent. But this time Twisted-stalk's heart beat suddenly a bit faster and his steps became lighter and quicker.

---

[22] By this time, some Indians had adapted to the use of log cabins, built as the white men had learned to do, except that usually the Indian cabins had dirt floors, and instead of a chimney, they simply left a large hole, in the center of the roof, so that the Indian custom of a central fire could be honored.

The laurel thickets were alive with cheerful songbirds. Long shafts of yet unfiltered light cut through the tall pines, bringing life to the budding understory. It was a tranquil, mystical scene—high—rocky—green—beautiful, a place of spirits and visions.

His intelligent black eyes danced from one familiar landmark to another. There, was the pool where he, Red-corn, and Solomon had caught speckled trout by the basketful. There, was the little cove, where the same three had sat so often close around late-night campfires feeding the flames and planning the glory of the successful war parties and lightning fast raids they would lead against their ancient enemy, the Cherokee.

Each tree, each rock, each flower, now welcomed him home. His feet remembered every dip and rise of the winding trail they now followed, in the late afternoon's light, of this warm spring day. From here the narrow path through the rhododendron would cross and re-cross the Raymondskill, following its splashing water always downward toward the river.

Below them, he knew, though he could not yet see it, lay the valley of the Minisink.

Chapter 36: Some Real Trouble

The morning sun shown hot but the wind blew cold. It was one of those sunny days when Manitou could not decide, whether or not, to let winter give in totally to spring. Red-corn, Twisted-stalk and the others had been in the valley almost a week. But none of their old neighbors knew they were here. They had been careful.

The War between the French and English was beginning its third year. The fighting had so far missed the upper parts of this valley. But the whites In the Minisink had not been idle.

A string of stockade houses and new forts dotted the landscape, from Peenpack all the way to the Water gap, and then southwest into Pennsylvania. These Stockades were built so that people could quickly move to them, for protection, when an alarm was sounded. Still, today, these folks were about their business, much like any day, tending their farms.

On the Pennsylvania side of the Fishkill old Tom Quick was cutting hoop poles near the river. The old man had cut three saplings when he felt a twinge in his chest, and decided to sit down for a minute. Fortunately a fallen log was close to hand and he plopped down on it to catch his breath.

"I'm not getting any younger," he thought to himself "No use takin' chances. I'll just rest a minute and then get back to it."

Here, out of the wind, he felt warm. He looked up at the sky. It was a clear blue-bird-day and over the river, near the Jersey bank, he saw a white headed eagle winging its way gracefully upriver, toward its nest. The giant bird carried a large fish in its talons. The old man smiled.

"Okay," he said aloud as if speaking to the bird, "let's get back to earning our keep".

He pushed himself up slowly to return to his work. He pulled the hatchet from his belt.

An arrow struck him in the chest and then another. He gasped for air but little came. He felt faint. Then he saw the flash of something to his right. The round face of a stone war-club hit him in the temple, as he turned, and the light of a bright day went suddenly black.

The old man was dead when he hit the ground. Instantly a brave was on him, turning him face down with a knee in his back. The knife sliced from the front of his grey head all the way around to the nap of his neck. A fist full of grey hair was seized and yanked. The scalp was ripped from back to front in a very efficient manner. The old man's skin made a funny little pop as it came free.

A primal war-whoop rang out, crisp and clean, across the river bottoms. A long moment of silence followed. Then the birds returned to their song.

Tom Quick Jr. heard the war-cry from his father's killer. He recognized the sound. He froze in his fear. He was two hundred yards down river from old Tom. But after a moment he started to move toward the sounds of the trouble.

Then through the willows, he could see a dozen or more braves running now toward him. There was little he could do alone. If by some miracle his father had escaped, he would steal away, and they would reunite later, but for now, young Tom knew—he must run.

And so, he ran. Without even taking time to shoot the musket he carried, he ran. This was no time for hesitation. He must get shed of these boys quickly. He ran.

As he ran, the truth settled upon him. He felt shame, responsibility and grief. He felt helplessness, hatred and fear. There were no drums pounding and no chants being sung, other than his pounding heart and the returning bird songs.

The sun still shone hot on the valley, and the wind still blew cold. A hawk rode the thermals high above, as he often did. But, in the instant after the war-whoop rang out that morning, the Valley of the Minisink had changed. It would never be the same.

Young Tom Quick was a strong runner and a good woodsman, so he was successful that day in eluding his enemy. When it was over, and he was safe among his friends, he could not remember exactly how he had evaded his enemy. But he knew who the enemy was. He hated them all. He intended to make every last one, pay for what they had done.

Chapter 37: Decisions

The sleet had stopped. The air was colder. Light, dry, snowflakes were beginning to fall. Outside Cole's Fort there was a foot of late spring snow cover. Inside, the ground resembled a sheet of dirty brown ice. The snow had been packed solid by the treading of many feet and hooves.

Where fires had been kept burning, there was a dark ring of brown, thawing mud. This muck had been tracked a thousand directions by the inhabitants as they moved from chore to chore, or sometimes, when they just wondered aimlessly, from place to place, trying to stay warm.

Daniel and Jakey huddled together on the narrow elevated walk boards, attached to the inside of the southwest palisade. Six foot tall, eighteen-year-old Daniel had outgrown his twenty-one-year old brother. Daniel had the big broad shouldered build of the Davids clan. Jacobus, resembling more the Decker side of the family, was half a foot shorter, a good sixty pounds lighter, with sharper more angular features. The boys were different in other ways too, but they were brothers. Anyone with an eye could see that.

Most frontier families grew up being never far apart. Brothers developed identifiable patterns of speech and movement, which seldom changed once established. An experienced eye from the community could often guess lineage at a distance by simple observation.

Few people, even had they been strangers, would have mistaken these two as anything but brothers. From time to time one of the two would cast a glance toward the tree line, which stood about one hundred and fifty yards west of the wall. Mostly, the boys watched a small group of women, who worked around a fire near the inside northwest corner of the parade grounds.

"Everyone calls it the parade ground," thought Daniel, "but there has never been a parade or even an assembly of any kind that I can recall."

"Ma seems more herself these days," said Jakey, nodding toward his mother working with the women at the fire.

"Yeah, she is almost back to her old self, I reckon," said Daniel. "It's been a while and I guess she has realized she can't cry for Pa forever."

"I never seen her cry all that much."

"No Jakey, she mostly done her crying at night, when we didn't see, but she did it—plenty."

"I know it. But, I'd have rather seen her cry instead of those blank stares she used to have."

"Yeah, and I was real tired of finding her sitting in the dark. It wasn't like her. I was afraid she might up and die herself."

"Yeah, this is better. She can't mourn for Pa forever."

Jakey chuckled to himself and nodded toward his mother again.

"It's good to see her taking an interest in her work. Look at her, a-bossin' them other women. Ma sure likes to make soap. Don't she?"

"But what she likes about it, I can't figure. It's always a galdern mess as far as I can see. She used to get downright mean, if any us children got close, when she was a blending it or leaching the lye."

"That lye will burn you boys bad, she'd yell."

The brothers laughed.

"Yeah, I remember, and she was darn fussy about how we gathered them ashes from the fireplace for her lye making. She always wanted oak and hickory ash. She wanted it light and flakey, almost like it was a piecrust or something, remember? She sure didn't want no charcoal mixed in neither. She swore, one time, she was going to tan my hide if I didn't quit getting charcoal bits in the ash fer her leaching trough."

"She always had me tamp it down. But she would make me move back twenty feet, when she poured in the water, especially if it was the second or third wash. You know when it really got to sizzling and popping."

"I was glad, when I got old enough, to leave that to the yougins an go to work in the fields with Pa."

"Hey, what you boys up to?" came a call from below.

They looked down to see Uncle, Jorris, looking up.

"Watchin' Ma show those women how to make a proper batch of soap," answered Daniel.

"Well I reckon it's a good thing we had them hogs to kill last week," said Jorris, "else there wouldn't be enough lard fer no soap."

"Soap makin's usually done in the fall, but then I guess, so is the hog butcherin'. I reckon this Injin scare has got a lot of things all mixed up."

"Where you been Uncle Jorris?" asked Jakey.

"I just came through the Clove from over Deckertown way. Where's all the men folk at?"

"Mostly they're off and gone, out in groups, to feed livestock and tend to things needin done on the nearby farms." Said Jakey. "Major Swartwood went back up to Peen-Pack, and the Westbrook boys went back to Brinks Fort this morning. The Westfalls mostly ain't never come in yet at all. Simon and some of his kinfolk are forted up at his house, trying to protect their buildings and livestock. Their women and children are here in the fort, though."

"Where's the Jersey boys?" asked Jorris.

"One's over there at the gate. Another one there on the southeast wall" said Jakey. "The rest are in the blockhouse I guess. That Fegley boy rode out last Friday to go to Marbletown, fer some reason er another. We ain't seen him since.

Where's Old Jake, Uncle Jorris?" asked Jakey.

"Last I knowed, he was a goin to scout the Shawagunk Ridge. That was Thursday last I believe."

Jorris strode a few steps north and climbed a short ladder up to the walkway, then walked back to stand with his nephews and look off toward the west.

"Any sign of anything?"

"Nope. We saw white smoke off to the south, earlier. Figured it was Westfalls' breakfast fire. Not much since."

Daniel turned to face his uncle. "Do you think the Injins will trouble folks on this side of the Fishkill?" he asked.

Jorris shrugged. "The Munsi might stay on their side, but there's no tellin' now. No way to know who is in charge any more, what promises have been made, who exactly is out there. It may be the Munsi or Shawnee. But it might be Ottawa, Huron or even the French themselves. God help us, it might be all them and others besides. It all depends on who, and how many. And we still don't know."

Jorris paused, leaned over the wall and spat thoughtfully on the ground below, then he continued.

"The snow was almost gone. Then we got that late one right after old Tom got killed. Then it got cold again, soon as we all forted up. Maybe there ain't so many of them out there. Then again, maybe they're just holed up, like we are, waiting fer the weather to clear."

"Is Deckertown still growing like it was?" asked Jakey.

"Yeah, it's getting bigger ever day. Folks figure it's safer there than here I reckon. Lots of folks are movin on down into the valley of the Paulinskill, or up and over the Shawagunks to Goshen. Cain't blame em I guess."

"Don't hear much talk about the border tween Jersey and New York no more do you?" asked Daniel.

"No, most folks have kinda forgot about that trouble for a spell. I ain't forgot our business though," said Jorris.

"Do you think we'll find the man who done it?" Daniel asked.

"I don't know boys."

Suddenly Jorris heard a ruckus from the women around the fire. "What's that they're doin' now?"

"I think I heard ma say the soap was tracking," said Jakey. "That means they'll be ready to start pouring into the molds pretty soon."

"Yeah I guess so," said Jorris, as he returned to his thoughts spitting over the wall again.

"Will you fight the Munsi? Uncle Jorris." asked Daniel. "You and Pa was friends with em' once."

"Yeah, we were. I have some good friends who are Munsi" said Jorris. He looked toward the west and spat again. "But I'll fight 'em if they come this side of the Fishkill to do mischief. I won't go looking for trouble on their side of the river though. Others will. But I won't. Neither will OId Jake.

Jake tried, years ago, to tell them fools down in Philadelphia, that their so-called Walking Treaty was gonna lead to trouble some day. Well, here it is. The Munsi have sided with the French again' us. Now we all got to choose a side.

The greedy hotheads have got us up a war. Now that the blood has started to flow it will be hard to cork that bottle up fer a while. I'm afraid none of us will be able to sit it out, much as we might like to."

He spat over the wall again, and then pulled his knife from the sheath on his belt. Casually, and thoughtfully he checked the blade's edge by slicing a few thin, curling, slivers from a post of the palisade wall, then he put the knife back in its sheath.

"We will defend our kin, our neighbors and what's ourn—but we don't have to cross the big river to do that—me and

Old Jake have decided we ain't gonna. I hope you boys won't either. We might go north and fight the French and French-Indians, but not west to fight the Delaware, unless they cross to our side of the Fishkill."

"Where's your sisters, boys?"

"Lea and Belietje are in the church," answered Jakey. "They're spendin' lots of time together, before Jerimias moves Lea over to Deckertown with his folks."

"Well, Jerimias Kittle is a good boy. I guess he figures that's best. I'd rather have her here with us, but she's his wife now, and I guess he knows what's best for his family. When the baby comes I reckon he wants her with his Ma and sisters. I'm sure they will take good care of her and the youngin too."

"Boy, who would have thought, last summer, that Lea would be married today with a baby on the way?" asked Jakey.

"Yeah, and I think Beletie might be next," said Daniel. "She and that Fegley boy are spendin lots of time together at church on Sundays."

"Well boys, life don't stand still even during a War. Fact is, it usually speeds up, excepting fer them that gets killed. It's our job to keep up." Jorris looked again toward the soap makers. "Looks like them women are fillin the molds to cool and cure. In a week or so you boys can get a proper bath if the temperature moderates any."

※

Later that evening Jakey and Daniel were back on the wall. Most of the community work-parties had returned to the fort.

A pair of mallards appeared suddenly, winging their way from the Fishkill northward, likely headed toward some familiar nearby bend in the Machackemack River. As soon as they cleared the tree-line, they saw the newly built fort. The ducks quacked excitedly a few times, and began gaining elevation quickly. When they passing over the boys there were sounds of much air being pushed behind, their rapid wing-beats.

The sun had just passed below the western ridgeline, and the dimming light made it seem cooler. But, a warm southerly breeze had blown in during the afternoon. It portended the beginning of spring more than a continuation of winter.

Pop! ... Pop! ... Pop!-Pop!

"Muskets!" said Jakey as he watched the southwestern tree-line with a new intensity.

"Far off. But not too far," said Daniel, "Maybe at Westfalls."

Pop! ... Pop!-POP!-POP!

"Yeah, them's not hunters. There's a fight going on. That's sure."

Soon a dozen men were on the wall looking southwestward. Jorris stood with his nephews.

Pop!... came another muskets report.

"They're coming one at a time now," said Jorris. "The surprise is over. Both sides are settling in for the siege. As long as we hear one at a time, like that, we can assume the Westfalls are still holding out. Unless Westfall and his boys were overwhelmed right at the beginning. If that's the case, it's just the Injins pretending a siege, while they set a trap fer us. If we send out a rescue party, they may be waiting on us. There's no way to know for sure."

Jakey and Daniel pulled their eyes away from the tree-line to look at each other momentarily, then back at their Uncle. They were worried and Jorris saw the fear.

"After dark, I'll slip over the east wall and scout my way around to the north and west. I'll come southwest and cross the little river near carpenters point, then I'll come up on Wetfalls place from the Fishkill side, for a look see. Nothin' to do till then, but keep a sharp eye and listen."

Pop! Came the sound of another musket shot.

"I hope Simon and all his boys were close to the house when the shootin started."

In the darkness, Jakey and Daniel stood on the walkway of the northeast wall, holding their Uncles long-rifle, bullet pouch, and powder horn. Jorris was lowering himself over the forts palisade wall, using a large rope he had knotted for the purpose. He let himself down silently and stepped his moccasined feet to the ground, with the sound of a cat, instead of the thud of one hundred and sixty pounds dropping ten feet to frozen earth.

Jakey tossed down his powder horn and bullet pouch. Jorris flung them crisscrossed over his shoulders. Daniel tossed down the rifle. His uncle caught it, with a swinging catch, to cushion the impact.

In half a dozen quick steps Jorris Davids, disappeared into the shadows.

"How long will it take him to circle round Jakey?"

"Three, maybe four hours. It ain't something you want to rush. Uncle Jorris knows what he's doin."

"So do the Indians Jakey."

Daniel gazed into the darkness.

"Yeah," said Jakey. "Well, uncle Jorris is even more careful when it's Indians he's stalking. He'll be back. But maybe not till morning."

There was only a quarter, waxing moon when it rose. Clouds often covered what little light it offered. The distant gunfire had slowed to one or two shots per hour. Inside the fort some folks were trying to get some rest.

But all the Westfall women were on the wall along with most of the Decker and Cole families. The women stared into the night as if they could see through darkness. They jumped involuntarily with each and every musket report when it came reverberating across the distance.

About five-of-the-clock in the morning, what moon there had been slid down behind the Pocono Ridge and it was darker still. A few minutes later a dim light began to show on the horizon. Daniel thought the dawn had finally arrived. Then he remembered. He was looking south, not east.

"Fire!" whispered one of the Westfall women standing nearby. "They've set fire to something!"

Suddenly every eye on the wall was riveted to the growing light on the horizon. In a short time the blackness of pre-dawn, was lit clearly by a huge, dark, red, glow on the southern skyline.

The cheerless illumination was enhanced by reflecting off low hanging clouds. Those clouds had rolled over the Poconos during the night along with a strong southerly breeze. Soon the smell of wood smoke hung everywhere in the air.

"The devils have fired the barns," one of the women gasped. Then, after a moment's thought, she added, "the animals are in the barns."

There was weakness in her voice. She knew there was nothing anyone could do, but watch.

※

Nearer the Westfall farmstead, Jorris Davids could hear the terrified, frantic screams of the horses and cattle, as they burned to death in the barns. But there was nothing he could do to help them.

Shouts, curses, and a few musket shots rang out from the fortified stone house. The Indians and Frenchmen responded with ugly mocking laughs returning the insults and the lead.

From inside the house, the defenders could see little past the burning barns. The attackers lay beyond hidden by the darkness.

But, Jorris suddenly had quite a good view. Because the foe had stationed themselves in the woods, between he and the burning barns, they were, for him, clearly silhouetted now against the backlight of the burning buildings.

He could see the savages, moving cautiously among the trees, across a sharp, deep, ravine. He could hear their arrogant laughter, whenever the Westfalls' musket-fire missed its intended targets. The enemy braves and the Frenchmen were spread out along the base of a little rise, upon which the barns sat. The stone house was up slope beyond.

It took a while, but Jorris was able to count nearly a dozen warriors. He could see them slinking scurrilously about, out in front of him. From the sounds of gunfire, on the far side of the house, it was clear to him that the Westfalls were surrounded. Jorris estimated the whole war party attacking were likely only two or three dozen strong.

"If there are no more in the area," he thought, "these boys will break it off at dawn and get on back across the Fishkill. If there are more, they will continue the siege. We had best stay inside the fort, till we can do more scouting. I know all I need for now. I better work my way quietly back to the fort."

But, just as he finished the thought, one of the more impetuous demons jumped up, near a tree, directly opposite him, across the ravine. The man was clearly revealed, back-lit against the dancing dark red flames. The Indian raised his rifle above his head and screamed a loud, taunting cry toward the house.

Before taking time to think, Jorris lifted his rifle, pulling its hammer-lock back as he did, took aim, pulled the set trigger, and carefully squeezed the firing trigger, all in two seconds time. "Swoosh, BAAAm!"

The pan flashed and the rifle roared, with a foot of orange flame flashing out its muzzle. Through the smoke he saw the brave lurch forward, as the bullet struck home, breaking the man's spine. But Jorris Davids did not wait to see more, he was already running toward the fort.

"I shouldn't have done that!" he thought.

"Now I'll have to run. If there are others between me and the fort, they will skin me alive before tomorrow's sunrise. And they will enjoy doing it. What the devil was I thinking?"

As the dawn came, the air not only smelled of wood smoke but there was ash blowing in with the wind from the southwest. Daniel turned to look eastward toward the sunrise, the front gates opened slightly and Uncle Jorris slipped in, before the gates were closed behind him with a thud.

Jakey and Daniel jumped down from the wall and ran toward him. Soon there were thirty men gathered around Jorris.

"Boys we should have an idea where we stand soon enough. There are two to three dozen of the enemy surrounding Simon's place. The Westfalls seem to be holding well inside the stone house.

I'm guessin the savages won't break off the siege, unless they're the only ones this side of the big river. If they get gone by breakfast, then maybe there ain't so many around. That's my theory. But it will take more scouting today or maybe tonight to be sure. Nothin more to do now but keep watch and get some rest."

Quickly the men melted away to find a place to sleep. Jakey and Daniel stood alone with their uncle.

"Did you see the Injins up close Uncle Jorris?" asked Daniel.

"Yeah boys, I did," he said.

"I guess our decision is made." He cleared his throat and spat thoughtfully on the ground. "We've got our answer. They're on our side of the river, so they're the enemy. I killed one tonight. I sure hope it weren't one I knowed."

Chapter 38: Back Across the Fishkill

Daylight was showing along the Kittatinny Ridge. The war party was leaving the burning barns behind and trotting off, single file toward the river. They were tired, hungry and frustrated. This raid had not gone as well as they had hoped.

Red-corn noted that the half dozen Frenchmen, among them, seemed pleased. But he wasn't sure why. They had taken no scalps and no plunder. What was there to be pleased about?

Red-corn was perplexed, at the French behavior, but happy in his heart to be leaving. He had not been in favor of this attack and he had taken no joy in the screams of the animals burned up in the barns. The Munsi, in general, had been reluctant to cross the river and attack the white settlers at Minisink. But the Frenchmen, whom they had joined forces with two days before, had insisted.

The Huron warriors, the French had brought with them, had chided the Delaware Indians, calling them old women. After only a little of this harangue, the young warriors among the Delaware joined in and the wiser men had been persuaded, against their better judgment, to come along.

Now, as they arrived back at the river, a startled great blue heron rose slowly, with a "cronk" flapping long angular wings, and gracefully winged its way upstream. Red-corn looked at Twisted-stalk. His friend wore a face, which did not smile but told him all he needed to know.

Both Red-corn and Twisted-stalk were happy to be heading back to their side of the river, not having shed any blood of former friends. They wanted to be fighting Pennsylvanians, and they were anxious to be about that business, west of the Fishkill, preferably further south, where most of the trouble making white men had come from in the first place. Perhaps with French help they could someday even attack Philadelphia.

Twisted-stalk noticed his friend's glance and knew its meaning.

The war party quickly began heaping their weapons, clothes, and powder-horns onto three small log rafts, waiting by the water's edge. Peeling off their moccasins they added them to the pile. The French Lieutenant grunted, and waved a hand toward the far side of the Fishkill. Naked, they pushed the rafts into the river, waded out to deeper water and began swimming toward the west bank, slowly pushing their rafts ahead of them.

The water was cold. Twisted-stalk tried to think of happier, warmer times when he had swam across this river. But his thoughts kept returning to the present.

"The only good thing about this raid," he thought to himself, "is that the one warrior killed was that loud mouthed Huron. I did not like him anyway. In fact I don't like any of the Huron. They are crude people. The French use them like dogs to do their hunting."

But I do like the Frenchmen. They seem a happy lot, for the most part. They are fair in their trading. They live in the woods as well as we and they treat us with respect. The French are the enemy of the English. They will help us defeat the Pennsylvanians and we will return to the lands of our grandfathers."

The water was cold. Twisted stalk took in a big gulp of water—choked a bit—coughed it up—spit it out, then went back to his thoughts.

"In summers yet to come my grandchildren will swim this river on warm sunny days, and laugh, and fish for shad, and be happy."

He smiled at that thought and began kicking harder against the cold water, to fight off the numbness slowly creeping up his legs.

Chapter 39: What's to Be Done?

The sun was at its zenith. A lone figure emerged from the forest one hundred fifty yards out in front of Coles Fort. The man was hunched over, carrying a musket, and running toward the gate. He glanced over his shoulders every few steps as he ran. It was Simon Westfall.

The gates opened as he came up and like a mouse entering a pantry Simon slipped in. The gate closed quickly behind him. On his approach the call had gone out across the parade ground. Now as he came inside the Westfall women came pushing through the crowd of men. They intended to hear what he had to say.

Simon paused to catch his breath. One of the Jersey boys handed him a dipper of water from a bucket kept by the gate. He grabbed the dipper and gulped at it, till the water was mostly down his parched throat but with more than just a bit dripping from his chin whiskers. Then he turned to embrace his wife and face the others of his family and neighbors.

"Everyone is okay at the house. Zack was shot in the butt. The bullet went through without hittin bone. James caught a splinter close to his eye, but he'll be alright. Andrew sprained an ankle getting into the house. Otherwise nobody else is hurt. They're all still forted up."

"I scouted, best I could, getting here. I believe the savages have crossed the big river back into Pennsylvania. Unless there are others about, they'll move on, now that we know they're here. We'll have to risk some scouting, the next couple days, but I believe the worst is over, for now."

"Two riders, comin' in!" came a call from the wall.

The sounds of hooves clattering up the road were suddenly clear to all. The gates were swung open in anticipation of their arrival.

"It's Old Jake and that Fegley boy," came down the call just as the two horsemen cantered in and drew reign.

Jacob jumped from his horse and led it immediately to a nearby water trough. Old Jake dismounted too. But his older, stiffer joints took a bit more time and effort to get the job done. He looked tired.

Jacob returned and took the reins of Jakes horse leading it to the trough. One of the men in the crowd handed old Jake the dipper, which had been refilled from the bucket.

"Thank ye," said the old trader before he took a long slow drink, emptying the dipper. He handed it back to the man and it was quickly filled again and passed to Jacob.

"Boys," said Old Jake. "I been all over the Shawagunk ridge this past week and I seen no sign of trouble from that direction." He looked off toward the tall ridge to the East.

"I can't say fer certain but I don't think there is anybody roamin' around up there right now. If I ain't mistaken, I heard muskets a-firin' down this a-way from my camp last night, so I was careful comin' in. I run into Jacob here comin' back from Marbletown by the long way about through Goshen. He just come down the road from Fort Gardner this mornin'."

Jacob stepped forward clearing his throat.

"Didn't hear of any trouble up north," he said. "I had documents to carry to Goshen. Then, on my way here, I spent last night at Fort Gardner. They have seen no trouble there and were unaware of any troubles here. Jake caught me on the trail and we scouted to the southeast as we came in. Didn't see nothing there neither."

William Cole, Abraham Van Aken, and John Decker were the true leaders of the community sheltered inside this fort. Regardless of Corporal Ward's New Jersey commission to command the Jersey Boys at this post, everyone really looked to the old patriarchs, for leadership. William Cole glanced now at Ward, and Corporal Ward looked back; then he looked down at the ground.

"We'll send out six scouts tonight," said Cole in a firm voice, measuring each word.

"If they find nothing, we'll send Jacob south, to headquarters with the news, in the morning. Then we'll put six more scouts out tomorrow and if they find nothing,"

He paused looking to Decker and Van Aken. Each man nodded back.

"We'll announce the 'all clear' and everyone can go back home, if they want to. Till then get some rest if you can, we need men awake on the walls in the dark not during the daytime."

After the crowd melted away Belietje watched Mr. Cole, Mr. Van Aken, and her grandfather Decker amble into the church.

"They're all showing their age today," she thought.

The church was dark inside and none of the old men bothered to light a candle. They just left the door open and settled down on one of the back benches where they could talk.

"I expect the boys are right," said Willem. "The devils are probably miles downriver in Pennsylvania already. They've stirred up enough trouble here, to scare folks to death. Many will be lookin' to move back east of the mountains.

The French know what their doin'. They hit and run rather than stand and fight. That way they can get the most terror with the least effort, and with the least risk, to their own sorry hides. They know we got to get our crops planted if we're to stay here next winter. They'll be back later on fer another bite."

"Yeah," Decker grunted. "They'll sure enough be back in the fall, so they can burn our crop, or hit us again when we are busy with the harvest."

Abraham was thinking quietly before he spoke, and the other two suddenly looked at him, with a question in their eyes. He cleared his throat preparing to speak.

"Do you think we're doin right, keepin the women and children here?" he asked.

"Well we ain't keepin' no one!" John Decker sparked. "Every man makes his private decisions about his own family. Some may want to send their women and children east. Deckertown isn't that far, and my boys and kin over there will welcome anyone who wants to come."

The door had been blown closed gradually by the wind and it was getting dark inside the church. John Decker used his arms and hands as much as his legs, to pull himself up, but he got himself standing. He straightened his back with a sigh and took a couple steps forward to pushed the door open again.

"Some of my sons are determined to stay here and farm the place like we always have. Fer now, their women folk want to stay too." He paused, looking down at his old friends.

"Maybe the Red-coats will make quick work of them frogs, up north, and take the pressure off of folks here abouts." He pushed the door open a bit wider and stood looking out over the little fort.

"We'll have to start scouting farther out, and on the west side of the big river too, so's we don't get any more surprises. Otherwise we'll work the farms together and keep some of the boys always on guard. It's all we can do unless we want to leave everything we've built and skedaddle. I don't think any of us want to do that. Do we?"

※

Later that day Belietje Davids stood at the church steps talking quietly with her sister Lea. Belietje was worried.

She had never personally known any Indians. Unlike her father and uncle, she had not lived among them when she was young. The Munsi had been forced to move away the same year she had been born. In her life she had seen small bands and individual Indians on the trails but she had never really known them. And, she had never feared them either.

Now things were different. These Indians were threatening her family and friends.They were allied with the French. She knew that her grandfather Davids had always hated the French. She had forgotten exactly why. She wasn't sure how she should feel.

Off, toward home, Belietje heard crows calling. She saw them then. There were six, chasing a big owl this way, across the sky, no doubt toward the tall pines of Peters Point where the owl was hoping for refuge.

"The Indians are hard to figure," she said to Lea.

"But there's no reason, why anyone but a savage would burn up dumb animals in a barn, or try to shoot peaceful farmers, who are minding their own business on their own land." She didn't quite hate all Indians yet, but she was becoming afraid and angry.

"Well, I hate em!" hissed Lea.

"I don't care how many Pa and Uncle Jorris used to hunt with. I hope the boys kill em all."

Belietje was surprised at the rage she saw in her sister's deep blue eyes.

"I recon she's worried about her husband and the new baby that's a comin'" she thought. "I know she don't want to have to go to Deckertown and leave us all here. But I've never seen her like this before."

The cawing-crows were chasing the owl, still this way, circling out and then darting back in at the larger bird, making pass after irritating pass, annotated by their screaming battle-cries.

As she thought about her sister's reaction, Belietje watched Jacob Fegley, across the parade grounds. Standing near the block-house he was slowly and carefully brushing a bay colored horse.

Lea, calming her thoughts, noticed her sister's gaze. She smiled.

"Pretty ain't he?" she asked.

"Who!" snapped Belietje.

"Why that big, bay colored stud," Lea said. "Who did you think I was talkin' about?"

"Never mind!" Belietje responded.

"Oh don't be that way," said Lea with another smile. "I know you was watchin' that Fegley boy, though I don't exactly see why. I'd think young William Cole would make a better pick or even Jan Van Aken. They're both sweet on you and always have been. Their Pa's both have big farms too. Somethin' a gal needs to take note of."

"Well I ain't pickin' no one," said Belietje. "I'm just lookin'."

"Well you're a-lookin' quite a lot of late. You're startin' to appear like you're moonin' over him like he seemed to moon over you when he first showed up. There's been talk. Even Jakey and Daniel have noticed."

"Well, folks can stop their speculating. All I've done is be polite in church," said Belietje.

"Yeah, I know, but all that being nice and lookin' and talkin' is startin' to send out a message that some people are beginning to decipher, whether that Jacob Fegley gets the signals or not. If I'm wrong say so."

Belietje looked at her sister. Then she turned away to watch the crows chasing the owl.

"I don't know. He seems nice enough," she said. "He's got family over on the Paulinskill and more down northwest of Philadelphia. He's more a farmer than a soldier. Most folks round here seem to like him. Even Jakey said he ain't like the other Jersey boys—drinking and gambling all the time. He helps folks out with the farm work when he isn't busy ridin' off to deliver messages." Belietje turned back to face her sister, straight on.

"Simon Westfall sure likes him," she said. "He must have his reasons. Simon don't take to everyone. The more I talk to

Jacob the more I do kinda like him, I guess. He's witty. He makes me laugh. And he really likes babies. I guess a gal could do worse than that."

"Well all that ridin' off to carry messages is plenty dangerous you know. He may ride out someday and not come back."

"I know it—but he rides pretty good don't he?" said Belietje.

"I reckon he does," said Lea, furrowing her forehead and raising an eyebrow. "I guess I ain't noticed as much as you."

"Well I asked him if he was afraid," said Belietje. "He said he was but he figured he'd rather be mounted on a good horse if he had to run-in to any Indians or Frenchmen. He said that way all he had to do was stay mounted and the horse would do most of the work of getting away. I've watched him. He knows horses, and he rides real good. I guess he's in no more danger than the boys, when they go out to scout all over the hillsides by themselves. Everyone has to do his part. I reckon any of us could get killed almost any day in these times." Belietje said, looking off toward Jacob with a frown. Then suddenly her face lightened.

"But it ain't happened yet, and I'm thinkin' maybe it won't. This war has to end sometime."

Just at that moment, Jacob Fegley looked up from brushing his horse and caught her watching him. He smiled, bowing his head slightly in a greeting. Belietje blushed, but she did not turn away.

Instead, she tuned out the battle cries of the crows, just now arriving overhead. The two young people gazed into each other's eyes across the parade grounds of Cole's fort. Like two hundred and thirty-three other men, women, and children in the fort today, they anxiously awaited the outcome of the next few days and wondered just what this summer and their future might bring.

The End

Afterword

The French and Indian War would continue for seven more long years before a peace treaty. But trouble on this frontier would not end with that agreement between white nations. The political storms coming to the American frontier would last over sixty years and become known as the Indian Wars. There would be few blue-bird-days. When these struggles subsided the boundary lines between Native Americans and White Americans would be re-established. The new borders would end up so far west that no one had ever drawn these places on maps, when the trouble began.

The white colonists finally and quietly would settle their differences concerning the colonial borders between New Jersey and New York, but not before they had become states in a new country. The western point of the official boundary line between the two was set at Carpenters Point where the Machackemack (now Neversink) River meets the Delaware River.

The birth of a nation, like most births, was accompanied by great pain. There were winners and losers. But, spring follows winter. Despite the troubled times some families grew and prospered.

The people of the Minisink valley were involved in it all. Sons and daughters helped people the new nation. An unbending need for fresh land, pushed people always further west. Like John Deckers canoe long ago in the flooded Machackemack River, most families were simply swept along.

About the Author

The author holds an Associate of Science Degree from Vincennes University, a Bachelor of Science Degree in Education from Indiana State University and a Masters Degree from Southern Illinois University. He is an amateur historian and genealogist. He is, or has been during his life, an avid hunter, fly fisherman, mountain backpacker, canoer of rivers, farmer, antique collector, poet, husband, father, and grandfather.

Michael Phegley's love of the individual stories, which en masse make up our collective history, was sparked first in John Hodge's 1958 sixth-grade history class, Busseron Township School, Oaktown, Indiana.

The author lived for many years in the oldest continually inhabited European community in Indiana—Vincennes.[23]

The author traced his family roots in America, back to the eighteenth century Delaware River Valley described in this book. Phegleys (then spelled most often Fegely, Fegley, or Feagley) were always farmers. The author as genealogist was never satisfied with finding documents or cemetery markers. He had to locate parcels of land, stand upon those homesteads, and personally experience the natural surroundings his ancestors had so intimately known centuries before. That research, those deeply personal pilgrimages, and the subsequent questions awakened in the author's imagination, inspired and powered this story.

The author now lives with his wife and two dogs in Evansville, Indiana.

---

[23] Historic Vincennes was settled beside the Wabash River in the year 1732, by French fur-traders.

Bibliography

Hillman, R. R. (1934). Old Dansbury and the Moravian Mission. Stroudsburg, PA: Kenworthy Print Co.

Morris, L. (1852). Papers of Lewis Morris Governor for the Province of NJ from 1738-1746. 126-128. (W. A. Whitehead, Ed.) New York: George P. Putnam.

Multiple. (1891). Baptismal and Marriage Registers of the Old Dutch Church of Kingston, Ulster County, NY. 203. (C. U. Roswell Randall Hoe, Ed.) New York: De Dinne Press.

Multiple. (1915). Minisink Valley Reformed Dutch Church Records. New York: New York Genealogical and Biographical.

Multiple. (1915). Record of Minutes, Surveys, Stock Marks and Business Conducted by Precincts of Minisink and Motague 1737-1782.

Reading, J. (1915). The Journal of John Reading. *Magazine of History, Biography and Genealogy* , *X* (Third Series), 90-110.

Additional Sources

Title:	A Genealogy of the Quick Family in America (1625-1942) 317 years
Author:	Arthur C. Quick
Publisher:	Private publishing by A.C. Quick
Where:	South Haven, Michigan
When:	1942
Note:	(Located by this author at the Sussex Historic Society, Newton, New Jersey

Title:	Minutes of the board of property of Province of Pennsylvania, Volume I (Minute book H)
Editors:	John Blair Lynn, and William Henry Egle
Publisher:	State Printer
When:	1890
Note:	(798 pages, Available now online at Google books.) (Pages 661 and 662 recount the Commission of 1719 to establish the boundary Lines from the perspective of James Steel and Jacob Taylor who traveled with John Reading to represent Pennsylvania interests and returned to make report to the Pennsylvania board of property.)

Title:	A History of the Minisink Region
Author:	Charles E. Stickney
Publishers:	Coe Finch and I.F. Guiwits
Where:	Middletown N.Y.
When:	1867

Title:	"Map of Frontier Forts"
Author:	Jonathan Hampton
Publisher:	Not Published
Note:	Jonathan Hampton was Quartermaster for the Province of New Jersey during the French and Indian War. As Quartermaster he traveled throughout the frontier area and sketched a rough map of the frontier forts. It was his duty to supply these defensive positions and for that reason size of each installation, distances between, and topography were important and often noted.

A Copy of this map with some notations was made available to me courtesy of the Historical Society for Montague Township, Sussex County New Jersey.

Title:	Historic Markers of the Town of Deerpark and the City of Port Jervis.
Author:	Minisink Valley Historical Society
Publisher:	Minisink Valley Historical Society
Where:	Port Jervis
When:	1996
Note:	This is a guide to Historic Markers, which were installed many decades before. In the subsequent years some of the markers have been removed. Fortunately for me the ones designating the site of the Machackemack Church, the Homestead of John Decker and the Davids Mill are all still very much in existence.

Title:	Fifty Years on the Frontier with the Dutch Congregation at Maghaghkamik
Author:	Pauline Angell
Publisher:	Reformed Dutch Church of Deerpark
Where:	Port Jervis, New York
When:	1937
Note:	(This reference was particularly important to the writing of Storms at Kendiamong. I came across it first in the New York City Library Archives in Manhattan. It was early in my research and was just the spark I needed at that time. Although later research provided most of the story line for Storms at Kendiamong that later study might never have been done without the inspiration of reading Fifty Years on the Frontier with the Dutch Congregation at Maghaghkamik.)

Title:	History of Sussex and Warren Counties, NJ
Author:	James Snell
Publisher:	Everts & Peck
Where:	Philadelphia
When:	1881

Title: History of Wayne, Pike and Monroe Counties, Pennsylvania
Author: Alfred Mathews
Publisher: R.T. Peck
Where: Philadelphia, PA
When 1886

Title: History of Orange County, New York
Author: Russel Headley
Publisher: Van Deusen & Elms
Where: Middletown, NY
Date: 1908
Note: Pages 162-164 of primary interest to this work.

Title: Orange County History
Author: Edward Manning Ruttenber and Lewis H. Clark
Publisher: Everts and Peck
Where Philadelphia, PA
When: 1881
Note: Volume II pages 700-713 of primary interest.